Scene of the Chime

Josie Damico

Annie's®

AnniesFiction.com

Library of Congress-in-Publication Data
Scene of the Chime / by Josie Damico
p. cm.
I. Title
            2017962882

AnniesFiction.com
(800) 282-6643
Amish Inn Mysteries™
Series Creator: Shari Lohner
Series Editor: Jane Haertel
Cover Illustrator: Kelley McMorris

10 11 12 13 14 | Printed in China | 9 8 7 6 5 4 3 2 1

1

Liz Eckardt hummed as she opened the oven door. The savory scent of pot roast and vegetables filled the kitchen, and she closed her eyes, remembering family dinners shared with her adopted son, Steve. This was his favorite meal, and he always asked for it for any special occasion. She'd rarely had the chance to cook for him in the past several years, since he'd been in the military. Now that his tour of duty was over and he was home, she wanted to celebrate every day.

Sundays in the Olde Mansion Inn—the bed-and-breakfast she owned in Indiana's Amish country—were generally quiet and peaceful. Sew Welcome, the quilting shop that belonged to her friends Sadie Schwarzentruber and Mary Ann Berne, located on the first floor, was closed, and Liz had no guests at the moment, though that would change. A historic preservationist who had been hired by the town of Pleasant Creek to assess the clock tower for renovations was due to arrive.

Liz had little knowledge of the architect who had designed and built both the clock tower and the Olde Mansion Inn. It was about time she learned more about the history of the house she was living in, and this would be the perfect opportunity to do so. She'd talked with Bert Worth, Pleasant Creek's self-appointed historian and archivist, but even he didn't seem to have much information other than what was contained on the one-page history she already gave out to her guests who expressed an interest.

Liz heard a noise from outside and headed to the utility room to peer out the window. It might be Jackson Cross, the town's mayor, whom Liz was dating. Or maybe it was Steve coming early for dinner.

The gleaming black Chevy Silverado truck pulling into the driveway, however, was unfamiliar. She wiped her hands on her apron and headed for the front of the inn, hoping it wasn't an unexpected guest looking for a room. She'd never turn anyone away, but that would throw a monkey wrench into her dinner plans.

She had just gotten to the foyer, with Beans, her lazy English bulldog, following her, when the front door flung open and a man strode through as if he owned the place. Beans stiffened and barked at the intruder.

Kent McInerney was a tall man, with a sturdy frame that probably came from working construction. His thick graying hair was like a mane around his face, lending him the appearance of a fierce lion on the plains of Africa. Liz tended to think he cultivated that image, hoping to strong-arm people into doing what he wanted. She steeled herself for an upcoming unpleasant encounter. She had learned long ago in her former law practice to never show fear, and she wasn't about to be intimidated now. Kent, a local developer, had a reputation for bullying people in an effort to get what he wanted. And what he could possibly want from Liz, she had no idea.

"Liz!" he called out jovially. "Sorry to drop in unannounced like this. But I saw your car as I was driving by and knew you were home." His voice boomed and echoed around the space. Beans finally stopped barking and glowered at the man.

Liz straightened. "You caught me at an awkward time. I am expecting people for dinner."

He smiled what he probably thought was a genial smile. Liz amended her earlier assessment. Now he reminded her more of a shark spying a baby seal in the water.

"Well, I won't take up much of your time." He lowered his head. "Did I hear your son has come home from the military and has settled in town? I'm so glad he did well overseas, serving our country and making everyone proud. Now that he's home, you must be so relieved."

"I'm very proud of Steve, no matter what he chooses to do with his life," Liz said evenly.

He glanced around the foyer, pointedly avoiding the dog. "I can't imagine a young man such as himself wants to be stuck in a dead-end town in Indiana. He grew up in Boston, right? I'm sure he feels obligated to settle here, to take care of you since it's just the two of you. But there aren't a lot of opportunities for someone like him. Aren't you stifling his future here?"

Liz narrowed her eyes, suspicious of his motives. What business was it of his, anyway? "Steve hasn't made a decision on what he wants to do yet, but I'll support him, whatever it is."

Kent's face flushed a deep red. "I was just trying to be neighborly, seeing as how I am making an offer on the land next to you. You see, Pleasant Creek is on the cusp of a great opportunity. There are prime pieces of real estate for development right here, to help the town improve the economy and bring more people to the area."

He'd made an offer on the property next to the inn? Liz owned a good chunk of the frontage on this side of Jaynes Lake, but not all of it. Surely the neighboring landowner wouldn't sell to a developer. Would he?

"An offer isn't the same as a sale, is it?" She couldn't help making a little dig. This man really rubbed her the wrong way. "Mr. McInerney, please say what you came to say so I can get on with my dinner preparations."

He paid no attention to her request, taking his own sweet time getting to the point. "The Amish are quaint and a nice draw, but they're firmly stuck in the past. Pleasant Creek doesn't have to be. We need to propel this town forward and give the residents opportunities, especially the next generation, or they'll leave."

What an offensive man. "So, what do you propose, Mr. McInerney?"

He smiled again, assuming she was on his side. Nothing could be further from the truth, but she decided to hear him out.

"Call me Kent, please. We need higher-end housing, a development for those people who can afford to pay more and want to live in better houses than these rotting old places in town and on the farms. People like the historic feel of the town, the quaintness of the area, but they want modern comforts. I can give them that, right here on the edges of Jaynes Lake. It's the perfect location, far enough away from the manure of the farms but close enough to enjoy the old-fashioned feel of Pleasant Creek."

Anger flared. "You plan to build a major housing development here? You'll ruin Jaynes Lake."

He shrugged, completely unconcerned about her outrage. "And those people will shop in town and bring in more steady money than this town has ever seen, more than tourists could ever bring in. It will be an economic boom."

"What's the catch?" She heard the anger in her own voice and hoped she wasn't about to say something she might regret.

"You can help this town you love so much. Pleasant Creek needs *you*, Liz." His blustering tone was now softer, almost wheedling.

Understanding dawned and she almost laughed. "You want my inn and my land."

"Exactly. I'm prepared to offer above fair market value for the inn and all the property, leaving you free to pursue your life and your son free to pursue his own life. Here—maybe in one of my new homes, which I'll give you a break on—or elsewhere. You won't have to worry about having guests traipsing through your house to keep you afloat."

The man was insufferable. "I happen to enjoy having guests traipse through my house," she said.

He went on as if she hadn't spoken. "I think you'll find my offer more than adequate to serve your needs for a long time to come, especially if any of that New England frugality rubbed off on you from your time there." He pushed a piece of paper across the desk. "Think on it and let me know your answer. But don't wait too long. If you delay, the offer might decrease."

He headed for the door.

"Mr. McInerney," she called after him. "Please know that no matter what is in this offer, I have no intention of selling."

He turned back to face her, and something dark flashed in his eyes. His expression smoothed quickly and he smiled. "I suggest you think long and hard before you reject it. Keep in mind the good you can do for your friends in this town, and for your family. Good day."

The front door slammed behind him, the sound echoing through the foyer and around the rotunda. Beans barked again and Liz flinched. She was glad she could still hold her own with obnoxious people. She started to toss the paper in the wastebasket, but curiosity got the better of her. She unfolded the paper.

And gasped. The amount was staggering—far more than she'd paid for the property. Did he really think the Olde Mansion Inn was worth that much? But it didn't matter. No amount would ever induce her to support his plan.

No, a voice inside whispered. *It's not the inn he wants, but the land.* He would probably tear down this lovely old house and build a series of McMansions or condos on lots the size of postage stamps, completely ruining the charm of Jayne's Lake and the neighborhood. He wasn't trying to help Pleasant Creek—he was trying to help Kent McInerney. And Liz had no intention of being of any assistance at all. She ripped the paper into tiny shreds and tossed them into the wastebasket.

He had brought up one point that bothered her, though. What

did Pleasant Creek have to offer Steve? His friends were all back in Boston, although he probably had grown apart from them during his time in the military. There wasn't much in the way of career prospects here unless he was Amish or wanted to run a store of some kind. Would he really stay here just because he thought that was what she wanted? Steve had only been back a few weeks, not enough to really know what he wanted to do. She'd talk with him at dinner and see what he planned. Steve would *not* sacrifice his dreams to stay close to her—she wouldn't allow it.

The front door opened again and she whirled around, half-expecting Kent McInerney to be back to renew his demands. Instead, Jackson stood there, a smile on his face and holding a box bearing the Sweet Everything bakery logo. Beans trotted across the foyer, his stumpy tail wiggling in welcome. Knowing Jackson, there was a special treat for her pet in the box. Liz relaxed, but Jackson must have sensed her mood anyway. His smile quickly changed to a look of concern and he strode toward her, then set the box on a side table.

"Liz, what's wrong? You look upset." He laid his hands on her shoulders and peered into her eyes, worry creasing his face.

She tried to smile, but knew she couldn't hide anything from Jackson. "It's nothing. Kent McInerney stopped by with an offer to buy the Olde Mansion Inn."

Jackson's jaw tightened. "Did he threaten you? Kent is not a nice guy. And he's more than a little aggressive with his business practices."

She laughed, the sound a bit shaky to her own ears. "Well, he is definitely a larger-than-life presence. He told me that I was holding Pleasant Creek back if I didn't sell so he could build a housing development, and that new people coming to live here would boost the economy."

Jackson took a step back. "He's not wrong, but he's not exactly right either. Yes, it would be great to bring more people to the area and add a younger crowd, along with more businesses. But that would change Pleasant Creek. As mayor, I've fielded a lot of concerns on both sides from citizens, some who want the increased tax base and revenue, but few people really want to change the town from what it is. I knew Kent was looking for land to develop a new housing project. I had no idea he had targeted your area."

"He said he's made an offer on the land next to me. Jayne's Lake is a big attraction, I suppose. I certainly think it's beautiful."

Jackson snorted. "Kent couldn't care less about beauty. Only cash matters to him. But you're right, a lake could be a draw. Remember, though, that even if he does manage to buy the land it doesn't mean he can develop it. His plans would have to be approved by Planning and Zoning, not to mention the Wetlands Commission. There's no guarantee he will be allowed to build what he wants."

Liz shook her head and laid a hand on Jackson's arm. "I can handle him. Thank you for caring."

He pulled her into a hug and rested his chin on her head. "I'm here for anything you need."

She pulled back. "It *is* a lot of money. More than I ever imagined the inn was worth. But if I sold, what would I do? Where would I go? This is my business, my home, and the home of Sew Welcome. Sadie and Mary Ann are my family just as much as Steve is. I won't even consider selling. Unless you truly think I should, for the good of the town." She didn't see how anyone except Kent would benefit, but she had to say it.

He shook his head. "No way, Liz. This is your business and your decision. The inn is a vital part of Pleasant Creek and its history. You should do what you want to do and not worry about Kent, the town, or anything else."

She smiled, relieved to hear Jackson supporting her, although she'd known he would. As mayor, he would know if Kent's words were accurate about the economy and whether she was standing in the way of the town's prosperity. She didn't want to be the one to hold the town back, but she loved her home and was confident in her decision. Kent McInerney would never persuade her otherwise. She only hoped her neighbors felt the same way.

2

The pot roast was done to perfection, judging by the way Steve inhaled it later that evening. Or maybe it was because it wasn't Army food or something he had to cook for himself in the efficiency apartment he was renting. Either way, the three of them made short work of the meal, leaving no leftovers once they gave a bit to Beans. He was now snoring at Jackson's feet, quite happy to rest there. They enjoyed the cherry pie and freshly made vanilla ice cream that Jackson had brought from the bakery next door, then chatted about all sorts of things over coffee. But Kent's words still worried at Liz's mind. Finally, she had to ask.

"Steve, are you happy settling here in Pleasant Creek? I mean, your friends are all in Boston."

He glanced over at her, the familiar blue eyes and sandy blond hair—still in the buzz cut from the military—catching at her heart. It was hard to believe he was really and truly home safe. "Trying to get rid of me already, Mom?"

"No, never!"

He chuckled. "I know you're just making sure I'm happy. I thought about going back to Boston but, honestly, when I stopped over there on leave last time, it was too busy and too noisy for me. Most of my old friends have moved on to new lives. I don't have much in common with them anymore. I like the quiet and the peace that I'm finding here. Trust me, compared to Kosovo and some of the other places I've been stationed, this is heaven on Earth. I may not live here forever, but it suits me for now."

"Well, I wish you'd stay here at the inn. You don't need to spend all of your money renting an apartment." She knew she sounded a bit disgruntled and like a worrywart parent, but she had room for him at the inn, on the third floor. He could have the Sunset or Sunrise Room permanently.

He grinned. "Are you kidding? After sharing bunk space with a bunch of smelly guys, having my own place is a relief. And this way I'm not taking up a room that could make you money. I have enough saved to be able to take this time. I might go to college in the fall, maybe study business or something. I'm not sure. But for now, I'll look for some work, something to keep me busy now that I'm a civilian. Any ideas?"

Jackson cleared his throat and glanced at Liz a bit hesitantly. "Well, I wasn't sure about bringing this up but maybe this is a good time. We recently had a pretty big order come into the shop for some special mahogany for a custom high-end dining set. It should be delivered any day now. Remember that break-in we had a month or so back? This wood would be very attractive to a thief."

Liz stared at him. "You really think someone would break in again? I thought the police caught that guy."

Jackson nodded soberly. "They caught him, but fairly sourced mahogany can be very expensive, especially of this quality. I could use someone to act as a security guard. I was going to hire a security company, but I only need someone short term, for a couple of months while we work on the set. Maybe you'd be interested, Steve? It's mostly night work and would probably be really boring."

Steve shrugged. "So, I catch up on my reading and maybe figure out what I want to do next in my life. It sounds perfect, as long as you're not making up this job for me."

Jackson grinned. "Absolutely not. And I hope it *will* be incredibly boring and completely safe. You'd be doing me a huge favor."

Liz smiled at the two men in her life, happy to see them getting along. She had initially worried that Steve might not like Jackson or would feel threatened by him when he came back, but she should have known better. Steve was an adult, and Jackson was a wonderful man. Both were important to her, and it was a relief to see them enjoying each other's company.

"Well, there go my plans of getting Steve to live here." She gave them a mock frown, then grinned when they laughed at her. When it was quiet again, she added, "Actually, I had thought you could look at the third floor with me. There's a storage area up there where we keep a few cleaning supplies that I thought I might be able to clear out and expand into either another guest room or a studio apartment for Steve."

"Another guest room? I guess that makes sense. Why don't we take a look now and see what it would take to clear it out and expand it?" Jackson suggested. "I'll get my measuring tape out of the truck."

Liz stood. "Let's clear the table, and then we can head up."

Twenty minutes later, with the dishwasher loaded and humming away, they stood in the third-floor hallway, with Liz in the center of the doorway, and Jackson and Steve flanking her as they surveyed the storage space. It was a large closet, but now that she looked at it more closely, it was definitely smaller than she could reasonably refurbish into a guest room. She sighed. Maybe this wasn't going to work out quite as she had envisioned.

Jackson peered around the doorjamb. "It's kind of small," he confirmed. He eased past her into the space, Steve following close behind him.

Jackson sneezed and Liz grimaced. "I think we'll need to get up here and clean before we consider doing anything."

"And move those boxes. Whose are they?" Steve asked.

"I think these are yours. From Boston. I never unpacked them."

Steve raised an eyebrow. "I have no idea what's in them," he said. "I thought we left all my things over the garage."

Liz shrugged. "The movers must have split them up."

Steve pulled a Swiss Army knife out of his pocket. "I'm always prepared. Let's open these and see what treasures I've lived without for the last few years." He sliced open a box, then lifted the flaps.

He reached inside and moved some items around, then looked up at Liz and shook his head. "Nope," he said. "Not mine. I don't recognize any of this stuff." He stood and took a step back.

Liz leaned over the box, which emitted a musty smell. She didn't dig down in, but the top layer consisted of loose papers, photographs of people she didn't know, and a couple of books. She stood, wiping her hands on her jeans to get rid of the dust. "These aren't mine either."

"Who do they belong to then?" Jackson asked. He looked as curious as Liz felt. "Could a guest have left them?"

"That seems unlikely. If Sarah or I find things, we contact the owners and arrange to return the items or donate them, if the owners don't want them. I'd remember something this big. I wonder if they were left by the previous owners."

Steve shrugged. "Your guess is as good as mine. What are you going to do with them?"

"These items are old. They could be family heirlooms. I'll have to find a number for Nancy Redfield and call her."

"Make sure Sadie's not in earshot when you do," Jackson said. "There's no love lost between those two. Or Mary Ann, for that matter, though she's less vocal about her feelings."

"This was Nancy's family home, wasn't it? I heard she was going through a tough time before she left, and there were some hurt feelings in her wake."

"Well..." Jackson seemed to be framing his words carefully. "She and her husband, Jim, were in the middle of a messy divorce then. Neither of them were at their best."

Liz nodded. "I was a patent lawyer, but I've heard my colleagues who practice family law tell some awful stories. They always made me so sad." She tapped gently at one of the boxes with her toe. It seemed full and heavy. "I would have thought if Nancy was missing these items, she would have let me know by now, but I guess we'll find out in the morning."

Steve stared at the back wall of the room. "Jackson, lend me your measuring tape, will you?" Jackson handed it over. Without a word, Steve left the closet.

Jackson and Liz stared after him. "Will I ever see my measuring tape again?" Jackson laughed.

"I have no idea." Liz peeked out the door. Steve had gone down the hallway, past the Sunset Room and was just walking into the unfinished storage space on the other side of the house. "Let's go see what this is about." They followed him.

When they entered the area, Liz leading the way, they found Steve at the far end, measuring the wall. Their footsteps echoed around the empty room as they approached him. "What's going on, Steve?" Jackson asked.

Steve turned to face them. "Something doesn't seem right about that closet."

"Not right? What do you mean?" Liz asked.

Steve gestured to the door. "Guys, go back into the closet and tap the back wall, will you? Just humor me."

When they were in the closet once more, Liz shook her head. "I have no idea what he's up to." She knocked on the back wall.

"Do it again," came Steve's muffled, barely audible voice from far down the hallway. She complied.

Less than a minute later, Steve reappeared in the door. "Could you hear me? I tapped on the corresponding wall in the other space."

Liz and Jackson looked at each other. They hadn't heard anything like that.

Understanding dawned. "We should have been able to hear each other," Liz said.

Jackson nodded. "Unless this wall has been soundproofed, and that seems unlikely."

Liz pictured the layout of the unfinished space and this closet. "Both this closet and the other area are smaller than they should be, aren't they?" A frisson of excitement ran through her.

Jackson tapped on the wall again. The sound was faintly hollow. "This doesn't sound like a solid lath and plaster wall that would be typical of the period this house was built. It seems a little . . . flimsy."

Steve was grinning. He tossed the measuring tape back to Jackson, who caught it neatly with one hand and replaced it in his pocket. "I was nosing around in that unfinished space last time I was home on leave, and being inside here just now, well, something didn't seem quite right, square footage-wise. Are you both thinking what I'm thinking?"

"There's got to be a room on the other side of this wall," Jackson said.

A secret room? How could she have missed that in her own house? The possibility had never occurred to her, but then why would it? "This is crazy. It's like something out of a gothic novel. Why would someone do that?" The question was rhetorical, of course. There could be any number of reasons.

"Hard to say. There's no door, although the sound does change right about here when I tap." Jackson demonstrated.

"Someone might have wallpapered over the door to hide it," Steve offered.

Jackson nodded. "We could remove the wallpaper and see if there really is a door, or knock down the wall. There has to be some kind of entry into the space, either from here or the other side. I think there would be plenty of room up here to create another guest room and add another bathroom—though plumbing is expensive—and still leave room for storage, if you open everything up."

"Maybe Nancy knows something about this. I'll ask her." The possibilities were buzzing through Liz now and excitement grew in her chest. But she'd have to get an estimate from a contractor—not Kent—and run the numbers to see whether the renovation was a good investment.

Steve gestured to the boxes. "Do you want me to move these downstairs, Mom?"

Liz nodded. "You know, I think I do. Let's put them in my quarters."

Jackson and Steve each picked up a box. Liz closed and locked the door firmly behind them and they traipsed downstairs to enjoy the rest of their evening together.

———

The next morning, Liz was attending to some bookkeeping in the inn's library when she decided it was late enough in the morning to call Nancy. She idly sorted through some papers as the phone rang. Finally, a woman answered.

"Hello?" The single word sounded suspicious and cold.

"Hi, this is Liz Eckardt from the Olde Mansion Inn in Pleasant Creek. I'm looking for Nancy Redfield." Liz straightened in her seat, already feeling tense from the woman's tone.

"I'm Nancy. What can I help you with?" The voice hadn't warmed up one bit and Liz was reconsidering her decision to call.

"I bought the inn from you, if you remember. I found a couple of boxes in the storage closet on the third floor. I know they're not mine and I wondered if they were yours."

"The sale included all contents." If possible, Nancy's tone was even chillier. "I certainly don't have the time or inclination to go back to Indiana to take out trash. Feel free to toss everything. Or not. It's really up to you."

"Wait, Nancy. You left a few knickknacks and things here, some of which I'm displaying. But I'm talking about some old papers and photos, along with some books. Surely you want the pictures of your ancestors. I could send them to you."

"Our family wasn't close. Donate them to the historical society or throw them out. It doesn't matter to me. Is that all?"

Liz gripped the phone tighter, already regretting the call. "If that's what you want, okay. But one last question, and then I'll let you go. That storage closet . . . do you know if there was a wall put up at some point, partitioning it off? I think the room is smaller than it should be. Can you give me any information about that? I may be doing some construction up there."

Silence dragged, with only shallow breathing to indicate that there was someone on the line. Liz waited, wondering what was taking so long. Finally, Nancy spoke. "I never really noticed. We used the room for storage, but I rarely went up to the third floor. My ex-husband handled the maintenance and upkeep of the house." She cleared her throat. "I have reconsidered about those boxes. I would like to see what is in them." The woman's voice had warmed considerably, becoming almost friendly. "I miss some of my friends in Pleasant Creek. It's been a few years since I was back there. Maybe it's time for a visit."

Liz blinked, startled at the complete turnaround. "Well, I could have them shipped to you."

"No, I will come up there," she said firmly. "Do you think you could find room at my old home for me to stay for a few days this week? My schedule is clear so I'll be arriving in the next day or two. I'll contact you with more details." She hung up.

Liz sat back in her chair. That was a surprise. Nancy had gone from not caring one bit about the boxes or what was in them to suddenly wanting to make a trip to Indiana. Liz wondered how Sadie and Mary Ann would react to the prospect of Nancy waltzing around the inn again. Well, she'd find out sooner or later.

She looked up at a knock on the door. *Definitely sooner.*

3

Sadie stood in the doorway, a big smile on her face. "Morning, Liz! We have new fabric coming in today, just in time for summer quilting, if you want to come and take a look." She paused and cocked her head to the side. "Everything okay?"

Liz hesitated, trying to decide how to break the news to Sadie. It would have been far easier to tell Mary Ann and let her tell Sadie. But they were alone, so if Sadie flew off the handle, at least no one would see or hear it.

"I'm having an unexpected guest this week. A former . . . friend of yours, I think. Nancy Redfield?"

Sadie froze against the doorjamb for a long moment, staring at Liz. Then her eyes narrowed and she stalked across the carpet and fisted her hands on her hips. "What do you mean, a former friend of mine? Is this some kind of joke? When is she coming?"

Liz smiled. "Thinking of taking a vacation?"

Sadie shook her head vigorously. "Absolutely not. I won't leave you at her mercy. And I won't let her run me out of my shop again, not like last time."

Sadie and Mary Ann had always been rather tight-lipped about what had happened before Liz bought the inn. "Why was Sew Welcome closed until I bought it?"

Sadie sat down in one of the chairs with a long sigh. "Since she's coming back, I guess I'll have to tell you so you hear it from me, not from her."

"I appreciate that. You had a lease, right?" Liz prompted.

"Mary Ann and I had a lease with the Olde Mansion Inn for a long time."

"So why did you close shop? The lease would have protected you from any whims of a landlord." Liz smiled to let Sadie know she was glad she had them in the inn.

Sadie grinned back. "You should have seen your face when we first walked in that day with our fabric. I could just see the lawyer wheels working, trying to figure out if we were crazy, had a legal right to be there, or if it was worth throwing us out. I'm glad you let us stay."

"I'm glad you stayed too. I can't imagine the Olde Mansion Inn without Sew Welcome."

"We were Nancy and Jim's tenants for a long time, but she and I never quite saw eye to eye. She offered discounts on our material and quilts to guests without asking us. Made promises for us that we couldn't possibly keep. She even tried to increase the rent in spite of the lease."

"That must have been uncomfortable."

Sadie snorted. "That's putting it mildly. Oh, it wasn't always so bad. For years, Nancy and I were able to work together professionally, though we were never friends. It was just in the last couple of years, when she and Jim were having such terrible marital problems, that she started taking her troubles out on us."

"Well, I'll do my best to keep her from bothering you." Even as she said it, Liz knew that might prove impossible. Anyone staying at the inn had to walk right past Sew Welcome's door to get to the guest rooms upstairs.

Sadie smiled and shook her head. "Don't you worry about me. I can hold my own against Nancy Redfield."

"I have no doubt of that," Liz said. "Shall we have some coffee? I'll bring cups in for you and Mary Ann."

"That sounds lovely. Are there any of those snickerdoodles left from our last get-together?"

"There are." Liz laughed. She'd found that snickerdoodle cookies could turn around most bad moods. And she had a feeling she needed to keep Sadie in a good mood if there was going to be peace at the Olde Mansion Inn for the next few days.

A few minutes later, Mary Ann met Liz at the door of Sew Welcome. "I heard there was going to be a coffee break," she said, taking the tray Liz held and setting it down on the cleared worktable. "I could definitely use one, after unloading these new fabrics." She gestured around, then looked at Liz. "I also heard there's company coming," she said, pouring some cream into a mug, then topping it off with hot coffee and giving it a stir.

Sadie harrumphed. "'Company' isn't the word I'd use."

"Now Sadie," Mary Ann said reasonably. "You know we got the better end of this deal, when all was said and done." She smiled at Liz, who smiled back. "How much trouble can she possibly make?"

Sadie rolled her eyes. "You might be surprised."

"Well, I hope we're not." Mary Ann nibbled at a cookie. "Now Liz," she said. "How is Steve getting on here?"

Grateful for the change of subject, Liz and her friends settled in for a snack and a friendly chat. Later, after she took the cups and empty cookie plate back to the kitchen and cleaned up, Liz returned to the shop to ooh and aah over the new fabrics. A gorgeous deep-blue batik caught her eye. She could see it as the focal color of a Log Cabin quilt for Steve. But not right now. She had to be careful not to come on too strong, to let Steve find his own way and not try to hold him too close, as she wanted to. Somehow, making him a quilt seemed to be a bit too much right now. Perhaps it would be a good Christmas gift.

She heard a car pull into the driveway, and a couple of minutes later the front door opened. "That must be my guest," she said. "I'll catch up with you two later."

Liz headed into the foyer. A woman of about thirty stood there, dressed in a pair of black slacks and an emerald-green blouse, her dark-brown hair brushing her shoulders. Her head swiveled as she studied the walls and the woodwork, clearly entranced by the place, so much so that she almost bumped into a table. She laughed, an embarrassed blush coloring her cheeks.

"Sorry. I get a little wrapped up in my work sometimes. I'm Melissa Patton. I think Jackson Cross set up my reservation?"

Liz smiled. "Yes, we have you all set for the week. You're here to work on the clock tower?"

"That's the technical reason. But as you probably know, the same architect, Charles Lawrence, also designed and built the Olde Mansion Inn, which is why I was so excited to be able to stay in this lovely place. I hope you won't mind if I pick your brain." Her excitement was infectious.

"I wish I could help you, but I haven't owned the house long, and I don't know much about it. I can introduce you to Bert Worth, Pleasant Creek's unofficial historian. And coincidentally, the previous owner will be coming to stay for a couple of days. I'm sure she'll have more information, since the house was never out of her family until I bought it. I hope you'll share anything you find. This is all I know." She handed Melissa a copy of the bare-bones document she gave to guests who asked about the history of the house.

"You have such a beautiful home here. The Clausen family, who built the house and tower, were rather important in this town, I believe. I hope you won't mind me snooping around the house and taking photographs?"

"Of course not, as long as you respect my other guests' privacy. But I'm not expecting any until tomorrow, so you've got the run of the place. I've kept as much of the house intact as I could, including the woodwork. Except for the updated kitchen and plumbing I installed, of course."

Melissa looked pleased. "I wish more people were as conscientious when they redecorate. Most people are all about 'out with the old.' You can't imagine how difficult it is to strip paint off beautiful original woodwork. Or how much fine craftsmanship got ripped out and replaced a few decades ago when a less formal look was in style."

"If you find any old pictures or house plans, I'd love to see them, especially of the third floor. I haven't done much work up there and I'm considering some changes."

"I look forward to going over that with you," the younger woman said with a smile. "Which room is mine?"

"I put you in the Rose of Sharon Room. We can tour the rest of the house later today if you'd like."

"That would be great, thank you. Once I settle in, I think I'll check in with Jackson. We have a lot to catch up on."

"How do you know Jackson?" He'd never mentioned Melissa prior to this assignment, though Liz certainly didn't know all his friends and business associates.

Melissa laughed. "Oh, we worked on the renovation of a house in Bertram a few years ago. He did some of the furniture and millwork restoration while I advised to ensure the historic accuracy. We've stayed in touch, and he knew I was interested in the architect who designed the clock tower. I did my thesis on his work for my master's degree." Her voice was animated. She clearly loved her job. "So when it came time to have work done on the tower, Jackson called me. He's a good friend—well, a better friend to my husband."

Liz smiled back at her, pleased to have met the woman. "Will your husband be joining you?"

Melissa shook her head. "No, he has to work and we have a young son who is still in school, so they are staying home. I hope this will only take a week or so. I hate to be gone too long. Childhood goes too fast."

"I completely understand. It's hard to be away from family. I hope your stay is pleasant and comfortable. Let me know if there's anything I can do to make it more so."

Melissa picked up her bags. "Could you show me to my room? I'd like to settle in."

Liz took her upstairs and came back down to see Sadie in the doorway of Sew Welcome, watching Liz with a shrewd look on her face. "She's awfully young to be trusted with our clock tower."

"Jackson has worked with her, and I don't think she's as young as you think. I'll bet she'll be great."

"Jackson does know what he's doing, I guess. If he's worked with her and recommends her—well, that's all that matters."

Liz smothered a grin at Sadie's quick assumption that Jackson was always right. Though he usually was. And Melissa seemed like a lovely person.

Perhaps Nancy Redfield would turn out to be one too.

———— ⁓⁓⁓⁓⁓⁓⁓ ————

The next morning, Liz cleaned up the dishes after breakfast and then enjoyed a cup of coffee with Mary Ann and Sadie before Sew Welcome opened. Since there was only one guest, she'd given Sarah Borkholder, her Amish part-time employee, the day off.

Mary Ann placed a set of diagrams in front of Liz. "We're planting our flowers this year in an Indiana Star pattern."

Liz, along with Mary Ann and Sadie, had agreed to help sponsor one of the gardens in the park surrounding Pleasant Creek's clock tower. They had until the end of May to finish the planting of the flowers, annuals that would flower through September. If they missed their completion date, their patch would be disqualified from the Quilt and Garden Tour in Indiana.

"I've never done this before. How many flowers will we need?" Liz asked.

Mary Ann consulted her notes. "We're keeping it simple this year. We only need a few kinds of flowers and some turfgrass. Last year we had ten different kinds of flowers and almost eight thousand plants total. This year we need less because we'll be using grass as a filler for some of the lines here. About six thousand."

Liz groaned. "That's a lot of planting. I see painkillers in my future, along with a heating pad and maybe a massage."

Sadie grinned, her eyes twinkling. "This is why we break up the work among all of our customers. We've had the sign-up sheet posted for weeks. Opal and George staked out the ground last weekend so we can get started on the flowers at any time." Opal Ringenberg was a member of the Material Girls, the quilting group Liz belonged to with Mary Ann, Sadie, Naomi Mason, and Caitlyn Ross. Opal's husband, George, was a retired train engineer. Since the Ringenbergs laid out a corn maze at their farm every autumn, they could easily lay out a quilt design for a flower bed.

"Well, I suppose I have to show up and actually do some of the work. We can't hire anyone for this?" She was only half joking. The thought of handling even a fraction of six thousand plants was daunting at best.

"We won't do it all at once. I have shifts worked out. The flowers will be delivered according to the groups assigned. Sadie and Opal will oversee the organization here onsite." Mary Ann smiled.

"And I love to order people around," Sadie added.

Mary Ann pulled out some pictures of flowers. "Here's what we're planting. Purple petunias, orange and yellow celosias, and turfgrass to add the green lines around the block and through the center, to look like the seams." Mary Ann paused, as if a thought had just occurred to her. "We never even considered asking you for your opinion. I'm so sorry. Is this okay with you?"

Liz laid a hand on Mary Ann's arm. "Of course it is. I wouldn't even know where to begin with this job. I appreciate you taking it on and letting me put my name on it."

"Well, you'll put your money there too," Sadie added with a wink.

"And watch out for that one. She'll take advantage where she can." A woman's voice spoke from the doorway of Sew Welcome, the frigid tone dropping the temperature in the room by several degrees. She was an older woman, attractive, probably around Mary Ann's age. Her hair was dyed dark brunette and cut in a severe chin-length bob. She wore a pair of tailored crop pants and a matching top, with a designer bag and jewelry that didn't come from a discount store. She had money—or the appearance of money—written all over her.

Mary Ann stiffened, and Sadie's eyes flashed as she opened her mouth. Mary Ann laid a cautioning hand on Sadie's arm and gave a subtle shake of her head. Sadie settled for a glare, her jaw clenching tightly. Liz glanced back and forth between the women but quickly got to her feet and headed for the door.

"You must be Nancy. I'm sorry I wasn't out there to greet you. I expected you a bit later in the day."

The woman sniffed. "I got an earlier flight. I wanted to deal with this as quickly as possible."

"You wouldn't want to have to stay in this farm town longer than necessary," Sadie said.

Nancy lifted her chin toward Sadie. "Definitely not. I have better things to do with my time than hang around Indiana. Florida is definitely more my style."

"How's Jim?" Sadie asked, a hint of rancor underscoring her tone.

Nancy flushed. "You know perfectly well we're divorced. He decided to move to Myrtle Beach where the golfing is better. I prefer Boca Raton. I haven't spoken to him since the papers were finalized."

"I'm sorry to hear that, Nancy. It couldn't have been easy," Mary Ann said sincerely.

Nancy unbent slightly and nodded. "It was for the best, for both of us. I won't say it wasn't difficult, but we had grown apart and now we each have new lives. I'm sure he's happy."

Beans, hearing voices in the rotunda, came waddling out from the kitchen. Liz had wondered how he'd react to seeing his former owner and held her breath. Beans stopped in the rotunda, sniffing the air and studying Nancy. He plopped himself on a rug and went to sleep, either not recognizing her, or not caring.

Nancy looked down at him, then shook her head in disbelief. "You still have him?"

Liz was shocked. "Of course. He's a fixture here. The guests love him. And so do I."

Nancy shrugged. "He was always more my husband's dog. I thought he would add some charm to the inn, but he never really did anything more than lie around and cause more work. Oh well." She turned and faced Liz. "I was hoping to have what you're calling the Rose of Sharon Room. I looked up your accommodations online."

Liz couldn't believe anyone wouldn't love Beans, but the dog didn't seem offended. "I redid some of the rooms, so you may not recognize them anymore. And that room is currently occupied. I renovated the Heirloom Room into a suite, and I thought you might like that for your visit."

Nancy sighed. "I suppose. But why did you change the rooms? They were perfectly fine the way they were. Weren't they good enough for you?"

Liz blinked, blindsided by the sudden attack. "I upgraded the amenities and added some of my own touches, like any new owner would."

Nancy arched an eyebrow. "Are you saying that I didn't maintain my inn adequately?"

"Oh stop, Nancy. You know as well as anyone else that constant use on furniture wears out the fabric, and walls need to be painted or papered once in a while. You hadn't put any money into the inn in years. It's not your place anymore. Let it go," Sadie snapped in Liz's defense.

Nancy bared her teeth in a semblance of a smile. "You're right. The Olde Mansion Inn isn't mine anymore, thank goodness. You do as you would like, Liz. I'm sure it will be . . . charming."

The woman's words certainly didn't have the ring of sincerity. Liz wondered again if she had made a mistake calling Nancy. But she'd dealt with worse people in her time. She pasted on her best innkeeper smile. "Come with me. Would you like me to help you with your bags?"

"No, I certainly don't want to put you out." The women headed to the front desk and Liz procured a key, which she handed to Nancy. The sound of the front door opening and footsteps heading their way made both women turn their heads.

A figure appeared in the doorway.

"I should have known you'd try to sneak back to Pleasant Creek and not tell me, Nancy."

4

Nancy froze and slowly pivoted. "Jim. I didn't expect to see you here."

"Oh, this is starting to get good." From the door of Sew Welcome, Sadie rubbed her hands and almost giggled with glee.

Jim Redfield was a slightly overweight, balding man with a windburned and tanned face that most likely resulted from spending time on the golf course as Nancy had mentioned. His khaki pants were neatly pressed, and he wore a white polo shirt that strained over his paunch. He glared at his ex-wife, confirming that the divorce was not at all amicable and there were still feelings there—bad feelings.

Beans, for his part, wagged his tail a little but made no move to head toward Jim. Liz was relieved. Nancy had made it quite clear that she didn't want Beans, but what if now he wanted to leave with Jim? She needn't have worried. The dog seemed quite content right where he was.

Jim gave Beans an affectionate smile. "I assume you can accommodate me?" He glanced around. "It doesn't look busy. Any room will do. Unlike my ex-wife, I'm not picky. But I would like a private bathroom."

Nancy stalked across the floor toward him, practically snarling. "What are you doing here?"

He turned and looked up. She had a couple of inches on him with her heels. "Also unlike you, I have friends in this town. Friends who knew you were coming back. Now, I had to wonder why you would return to Pleasant Creek, a place you vowed never to see again. The only thing I could think of was that something must have come up with the inn, and the only thing that could have brought you here was money. And I'm entitled to half of whatever that might be. You meant to call me, right? But let me guess—you lost my phone number *and* my lawyer's."

Mary Ann looked uncomfortable, and Liz wished she was anywhere else. Sadie, however, seemed to be enjoying the show.

"Can we discuss this in private?" Nancy said through clenched teeth.

Jim shrugged. "Now you want to talk? After all our years of marriage, we never talked. It was always your way or nothing at all. But I'm more than willing to discuss the reason you came back to Pleasant Creek."

She glared at him for a long moment then stomped away up the stairs, dragging her suitcase behind her. Jim watched her with a small smile, then he turned and faced Liz. "I'd apologize for her but that's no longer my role. And I fear she'll do more things in the next few days to irritate you. Now, do you have a room for me?"

Liz shifted. She couldn't exactly turn away business when she had an empty guestroom. "I'll put you in the Somewhere in Time Room. It's on the opposite side of the house from where Nancy's staying."

"That's thoughtful of you. Now, why is she here? I'm a former owner too, and I should have received a call. But I'm not mad."

Jim squatted and held out his hand to Beans, who sniffed it and allowed a brief scratch on the head. The man straightened again. "I'm glad Beans seems so happy to be with you. He would not have liked moving with me and definitely not with Nancy. He belongs with the inn."

"I agree," Liz said.

Sadie and Mary Ann, sensing the drama was done for the morning, called a greeting to Jim and headed back into the shop, leaving Jim and Liz alone in the rotunda. While checking him in, she explained about the third-floor storage closet and the boxes. He frowned.

"I don't recall us doing any work there. I'd remember putting up a wall. I definitely want to take a look at it and the boxes."

Liz was definitely feeling very uncomfortable now. "Jim, I don't want to get between you and Nancy on this. It would be great if you two could work this out yourselves. I really don't want to be a go-between."

"Of course not," he replied genially. "She can be difficult at best. But I'm something of an expert in handling her. We were married for decades, after all. I know we don't look it. We were married right out of college. Big mistake. But that's not for you to worry about. If I have to, I can get our lawyer involved. Our divorce settlement was very clear." He hefted his bag. "Now, I'll get settled and check in with Nancy. I'm sure she'll want to see the boxes soon, and so do I. Would that be okay?"

"Of course," Liz agreed. "Just so you're aware, I have another guest on the second floor, and we have a fourth guest coming in today."

"Almost a full house. I'm glad to hear it. You seem like a nice woman, and it's good to see someone doing well with this place. I'll talk with you later." He headed for the stairs.

The tension was still thick in the air. Liz shook her head. The sooner the mystery of the boxes was cleared up and those two went home, the better.

———————— ///////////////////////// ————————

Later that afternoon, Liz's fourth and final guest arrived. Pete McConnell was a man in his forties, clean cut and affable. He wore jeans and a pale-blue button-down shirt and called her ma'am, making her feel much older even though they were close to the same age. But it was nice to have someone not adding to the stress, unlike the Redfields. Melissa had been gone all day, and Liz hadn't seen her until she had reappeared a few minutes ago and had gone to her room to change.

"I hope you don't mind the third floor," Liz said to Pete as she finished checking him in. "No one else is staying up there, and the rooms have a beautiful view of the surrounding area. I put you in the Sunrise Room. The bathroom is right next door."

He smiled shyly at her. "I'm sure that will be fine. I appreciate you finding me space at a reasonable price. I'm on a bit of a budget and thought I'd only be able to afford one of those roadside motels."

Liz laughed. "Pleasant Creek has a couple of those, and they're actually rather nice. But I try to keep my prices affordable. What brings you to Pleasant Creek?"

He shrugged as he followed her up the stairs. "I spent a lot of time with my grandfather growing up and got interested in my family history. I thought I'd come here and look up some of it."

Liz paused on the second-floor landing. "Your family was from around here? What was their name?"

He glanced away, as if he had shared too much. "Bieler."

Liz was surprised. "Your family was Amish? We have several Bielers in the area including a family across the lake, although I didn't think they had any children."

"Um, I don't think it's the same Bielers. It's a pretty common name in this area, isn't it?" He ducked his head and glanced around as if looking for a distraction.

Whether that's what he wanted or not, he got one. Raised voices came floating down from the third floor and Liz hurried up the last flight, concerned about the commotion, with Pete right on her heels. She emerged on the third floor to see Nancy Redfield and Melissa Patton face-to-face in the hallway, yelling. Melissa was not backing down from Nancy, and Liz had a perverse pleasure at seeing that, but she had to keep the peace.

"Excuse me, ladies. What's going on?" Liz asked, trying to infuse her voice with as much calming energy as she could.

Both women whirled, and she took an involuntary step back

under the force of their combined ire. She steeled herself and moved in between the women, forcing them to separate. Her movement broke their momentary silence, and both women started speaking, shouting louder and louder to be heard over each other. Liz exchanged a sympathetic glance with Pete, then raised her hands.

"Stop. Please. Now, Melissa, what are you and Nancy arguing about?"

"Why start with her? This was my house first," Nancy snapped.

Liz sucked in a deep breath, counting to ten in her mind and praying for patience. "Because I asked her first. Melissa?"

Melissa shot Nancy a triumphant glance, then folded her arms and spoke. "I was exploring the house, which you said I could do."

"I caught her trying to get into the storage closet. The door's locked, so that's breaking and entering. I don't want her here, Liz. I don't trust her."

That was an awfully big jump for anyone to make, particularly since the two women had just met. Melissa had more of a reason to be there than almost anyone else. And Nancy hadn't even cared about the boxes. Now she was overreacting about someone looking at them. It made no sense.

"Nancy, I'm sure Melissa meant no harm. Actually, I had planned on consulting with her anyway. Her knowledge of historic buildings, preservation, and the architect who designed this house might help me figure out the space."

"I forbid it." Nancy's words were sharp and rang out in the hallway.

Liz arched an eyebrow, her patience gone. "You forbid it?"

"Yes. Those are my things and I don't want anyone near them. It's bad enough you snooped through them. Who knows who else you let paw through my family's personal papers?"

"First of all, we don't even know they're yours. And second, you didn't want them when I called you about them. Why the sudden interest?"

"That's my business. Suffice it to say that I demand that no one have access to that room until I have time to review the boxes."

Liz shook her head. "I didn't even have to call you about them. Remember the sale was all contents included? That means that, technically, I own those boxes and whatever is in them. I'm trying to be considerate, but this closet must remain locked until we can examine them together." There was no need to tell anyone that the boxes weren't even in the closet, but were sitting on the floor of her personal quarters on the main floor, locked up tight.

Nancy opened her mouth but Liz held up a hand, staving off any more words. "I won't change my mind, so please don't ask. Meanwhile, Melissa, I mentioned Bert Worth as a resource for you. And Pete McConnell here, another guest, is also interested in some family history, so I'll set up time with Bert to come visit and talk with you both. Does that sound good?"

"McConnell? I remember a McConnell around here, but that was years ago. Were you related to a Michael McConnell?" Nancy asked.

Pete shook his head vigorously. "No, ma'am. My family was related to the Bielers."

"Hmm. I wouldn't have taken you for an Amish man." Nancy sniffed and kept her narrowed eyes on Pete longer than Liz thought strictly necessary.

"Well, my grandfather left the order a long time ago," he said, then looked at Liz as if hoping she'd save him. "Which room did you say was mine?"

Liz opened the Sunrise Room. "This one. And no one should be bothering you up here. If you hear anything, please let me know. You deserve a quiet area, and I will make sure you have it."

She gave one last meaningful look at Nancy and Melissa, then held the door open for Pete. He closed the door, leaving the three women outside in the hallway. Nancy glared at Melissa for a moment longer, then gave a sound of frustration and stomped off down the stairs. Liz gave Melissa a sympathetic look.

"I'm sorry about that, Liz. I was only looking around. Would it be possible for me to see in the storage closet? Jackson told me you think there could be some unexplored space behind one of the walls." Excitement threaded through Melissa's words and Liz smiled.

"I have no idea what to think. I was hoping you had some house plans we could check out to see what that space looked like originally, before I go to the trouble and expense of knocking down a wall."

Melissa nodded. "I left them at the town hall, where Jackson set me up with a temporary office. I should have brought you a copy. I'll bring one back for you tomorrow so we can compare. Now I'm going to change and head out to find something for dinner. Thank you for your help. Sorry if I caused any trouble."

"She has drawings for the house?" Sadie came up the stairs as Melissa walked down.

Liz watched Melissa disappear from sight, then responded, "It seems she found some plans."

"Do you think they'll give you an answer?"

Liz went to the storage room door and checked the knob, making sure the lock was still set. "I hope so. I'd like to find out what, if anything, is in that space."

Sadie made a sound of annoyance. "Is it really that big a deal? It's probably going to turn out to be nothing."

Liz took a deep breath and straightened up. "You're right. But I need to get this whole situation with the Redfields resolved so I can decide what to do about renovations. If the plans can help, then I'm all for it. Did you need me for something?"

"Yes, just letting you know I'll be spending the next few days away from the shop, supervising the planting at the tower. I think it's for the best, me avoiding Nancy Redfield. We're like gas and flame. So I'll see you at the garden for your shift?"

Liz smiled. "Definitely. Thanks, Sadie."

"Bring some iced tea. It's hot in the sun!" With those parting words, Sadie winked and headed downstairs. Liz sighed and followed her. The sun certainly was hot in Pleasant Creek, but it was starting to feel like the tempers at the Olde Mansion Inn had it beat.

5

The next morning, after Liz and Sarah had cleaned up from breakfast, Bert Worth bustled into the kitchen, his graying hair fluffing around his head and reminding Liz of an absentminded professor. He was a good, kind man who relished his self-appointed role as town historian. She escorted him to the dining room where he could spread out his papers. Melissa joined him and began to look through his offerings. Her excitement was almost palpable.

Liz returned to the kitchen to refresh the coffee. While she was brewing a new pot, Jackson came in and gave Liz a kiss on the cheek. "How have things been? I heard it's been a little tense here."

She furrowed her brows. "Tense? Who told you that?"

He shrugged. "Melissa might have mentioned her argument with Nancy Redfield."

Liz wiped her hands on a dishcloth and leaned against the counter. "Oh, right. Melissa seems nice."

He took a sip. "She is. Her husband and I go way back. She and I spoke last night about the tower renovations."

"What does she think?"

He smiled and put the cup on the counter. He pulled her into a hug, resting his chin on her head. "Does it matter? I'd rather spend time with you and not talk about business. Soon she might be dealing with Kent McInerney rather than me anyway."

Liz drew back. "Kent? Why him?"

"He's bidding on the contract to do the work on the tower and he'll likely get the job. I'm going to help with some of the millwork, but that's it. I'm just overseeing the initial planning stages of the project along with the committee." He released her and picked up his cup again. "We should have dinner soon, just the two of us."

"I'd like that. With all of this drama, I could use a break. A date night would be nice." She looked toward the doorway. "Let's go see what Bert and Melissa have for us."

Jackson followed her into the dining room, where Bert and Melissa sat at the table, which was now strewn with papers. "Have you found anything?"

"Well, we've compared Ms. Patton's plans and the ones I had in the town archives."

"And?" Both Melissa and Bert seemed excited. What had they found?

"They don't match," Melissa said. "Bert's are older—I think they're the originals—and we have a set of more recent ones, from when the house was renovated to an inn. So we have a great comparison."

Bert pointed to an older, more fragile-looking set of plans. "You can see that the third floor was originally the nursery and that closet was the nanny's quarters. Comparing the plans to the measurements tells us that the room is much smaller now, by several feet."

Jackson peered over his shoulder and nodded. "Which we suspected. What about the plans from when the house was converted? Was the room the same size then as it was originally?"

A broad grin crossed Bert's face. "That's where it gets interesting. The room is smaller in the new plans with no explanation. And there's a room on the other side that's unlabeled."

Liz frowned. "So when the house was converted to an inn by Nancy and Jim, that extra room was already there? Do you have any records at all about the family or the house to explain it?"

He shook his head. "No, the Clausen family didn't leave any papers to the town or the library. If they left any at all, it may have been to the state historical society. You'd have to ask Nancy Redfield. The house was in her family until you bought it. As far as I know, only one child ever lived here, so the nursery wasn't used long and was apparently converted to servants' quarters. Maybe it was divided to make room for more servants."

"I guess there's room for a twin bed and a dresser in what's now the closet, although it would be cramped," Liz said. "And someone would have had to walk through that little bedroom to get through to the next one."

"That's not at all unusual in old houses," Melissa said. "Live-in servants didn't have much expectation of privacy or convenience. You say there's no door there now?"

Jackson shook his head. "Assuming there is one, it's wallpapered over, maybe boarded up. If we take that down, we might find a door."

"How thick is the wallpaper?" Melissa asked.

"It would have to be a few layers of thick paper, if it could hide a door," Liz said.

"I wonder if any of the paper is vintage. I'd love to get a look at it," Melissa mused.

"No one is getting a look at anything. Not if I have anything to do with it." Nancy Redfield stood in the doorway, her face like a thundercloud. She advanced into the room and slammed a piece of paper down on the table in front of Liz. "This is a notice from my lawyer saying you can't let anyone in that room until I have a chance to go through everything. You can't touch the boxes, not even to move them. And you certainly can't let someone do any construction or demolition in there without my approval."

The room went silent. Liz snatched up the document and read it. Nancy folded her arms, a triumphant look on her face.

Liz shook her head. "This isn't right. I'll have my own lawyer look at this."

Nancy glared at her. "You can't do that. I have a right to that room and those boxes."

"So you say. First, you didn't care about the boxes, then suddenly you showed up and were extremely insistent that no one be allowed in that room while your things are in there. And then, after I agreed to show you the boxes, you bring me a lawyer's letter. I told you I'd let you see the boxes. You didn't need the letter. So why did you do it?"

"I wanted to protect my property." Nancy met Liz's gaze stubbornly.

"We have not determined they're even your property."

Nancy smirked. "According to my lawyers, since I was not aware of whatever's on the other side of that wall, it was not included in the terms of the sale. I have a right to review the contents, as they are personal items and not part of the inn contents."

"We seem to be talking about two different things here. One, the boxes, which I already offered you. And two, the additional space, which may or may not contain anything of value. You're not looking at anything until my lawyer reviews the sale documents and the legal demands in this letter. Until that's done, or you've got a court order in your hands, my word goes." Liz mentally shook her head. She didn't like playing hardball with guests. But this woman was leaving her no choice.

Jim stormed in. "What game are you playing this time, Nancy?"

Nancy whirled around as he stalked across the room to her. She backed up against the sideboard but lifted her chin defiantly. "This doesn't concern you, Jim. This is about me and my family. I'm a Clausen, and you're not. Those boxes, and anything in that walled-off room, are mine."

He slammed a piece of paper on the desk. "Not according to our divorce agreement. I am entitled to half of everything, not half of what you *think* I should have."

Liz, Melissa, Bert, and Jackson stared at the drama unfolding before them, apparently fascinated by this display of postmarital discord.

Nancy was not to be cowed. "This has nothing to do with you, Jim. For once, let it go. Get on with your life."

"If only it were that easy, Nan. I spent years being treated like dirt, like your lackey. You owe me this." He turned to Liz. "If I were you, I'd hide the key to that room and definitely consult your own attorney. Don't give in to her. She'll manipulate you and the situation. It's what she does best."

Nancy spoke slowly. "She has no choice. My lawyer has been very clear in this letter."

Liz folded her hands on the desk. "I will make my own judgments. The closet will remain locked until the matter is resolved."

"And my attorney will be in touch too," Jim said. "You won't get away with whatever it is you're trying to pull, Nancy. I'm watching you."

He turned and stomped out of the room, anger visible in the tense lines of his shoulders. Nancy sniffed and looked down at Liz. "I expect you'll keep others out of there?"

"No one will go in there until I can consult with my attorney." Liz was so tired of the arguing, the same fight over and over again. She wished she'd simply donated the contents of the boxes to the historical society and been done with it.

Nancy studied her for a long moment, then gave a curt nod and left the room. Melissa gave Liz a sympathetic pat on the shoulder.

Jackson heaved a sigh and stared at Liz. "Well, that was interesting. What are you going to do?"

"Exactly what I said I would do, although I doubt Nancy's letter holds any legal weight. I know the sale papers were solid. I wonder why she's pushing so hard on this. Do you have any ideas?"

Bert spoke up, craning his head around to make sure the Redfields were indeed gone. "I hate to spread rumors, especially when I don't have any proof. But it might explain what's going on."

Liz hoped Bert had answers. "What do you think?"

He looked a bit sheepish. "Well, awhile back, when Iris Clausen—this would have been Nancy's distant cousin—passed, there was a rumor that she had a fortune squirreled away in the house. A fortune that was never found or mentioned in her will. She had been the sole inheritor of her parents' money, and although she never worked a job as far as I know, she didn't seem to be a big spender. So it could have lasted a long time. Nancy and Jim Redfield lived with her the last two years of her life, and then Nancy inherited this house when she died. Iris left her most valuable historic furniture and things to the state historical society. But rumor has it that she didn't give away everything and that there could still be valuable items to be found."

"And you think Nancy is looking for them? Wouldn't she have found them before now?" Melissa asked.

"She lived here for thirty years," Jackson pointed out.

"But she didn't know about that secret room, did she?" Bert stated. "Not until you called her."

"That makes sense," said Liz. "She didn't care about the boxes until I mentioned the room. She does seem to be overreacting about a few boxes of personal things that might not even be hers."

Bert shrugged then stood. "I have no way of telling and no way to find out. But this is the grandest house in Pleasant Creek, and Iris was a bit . . . eccentric. So it's no wonder a rumor like that started. I suppose you can talk to people who might have known her then, but Iris was pretty reclusive by the end." He stood. "Time for me to get back to the courthouse. My display of town history needs dusting and I don't trust anyone else to do it. Melissa, I'll leave the plans with you. Just return them when you're done."

"And I'll walk over to the courthouse with you," Melissa said, gathering up the plans. "Liz, I'll keep these in my briefcase, but let me know if you want to see them again."

She and Bert left, chatting companionably, leaving Liz and Jackson alone.

"Is there anything I can do?" asked Jackson. "Maybe I can talk with Nancy, see if I can reason with her. She knows me a little better."

Liz shook her head. "No, I'll call the lawyer who handled the sale and we'll see what we can do. But I doubt she has a case. I know enough about this to feel confident about that. I think it's a bluff or they'd have gotten a court order. Do you think Bert could be right?"

"About something valuable being hidden in that room? I don't know what to think." He leaned down and kissed her. "Do you want to have dinner out somewhere tonight, to get away from the madhouse?"

She smiled. "I'd love that. Thanks."

After fixing a time for dinner, Jackson let himself out and Liz pulled the inn's sale papers and her lawyer's contact information from her files. She called the firm and explained what was going on, then made an appointment for later that day. Nancy was certainly being difficult, although Bert's explanation made a certain amount of sense, even if it was a bit far-fetched. The next time she decided to be nice and do the right thing, she'd have to reconsider. This had turned into a mess, and it seemed like the only way it was going to end was by knocking down a wall, whether she wanted to or not.

6

Needing a break from the tensions at the inn, Liz headed to town, hoping to spend a little time with Steve, maybe even take him out for lunch before her appointment with the lawyer. She dropped the letter off at the lawyer's office so he could look at it prior to their meeting, then headed to Cross Furniture Company.

Steve was sitting in a small space that had been set up as a security room, with computers and surveillance monitors to keep track of the areas surrounding the factory. He jumped to his feet, a broad grin on his face, when she knocked and opened the door.

"Wow, Jackson got this set up pretty fast."

He glanced around the room, a hint of pride in his face. "Yes, he had a lot of the cameras already in place. It was just a matter of redirecting them and consolidating the feeds here. It sure beats walking patrol."

She nodded, secretly glad that he was home and safe. "I thought I'd stop by and see if you were free for lunch. Weren't you supposed to be doing this mostly at night?"

He shrugged. "Well, Jackson got some additional wood in for the clock tower renovation and it's in his warehouse, which is deserted a lot of time. He'd like someone to keep an eye on it. So, I work a split shift, helping out at different times. I don't mind. It's not like I'm busy, and I find the work the guys do interesting."

Liz watched the different images on the screens. Workers were building furniture in the factory. She could also see the warehouse, which seemed empty of people, and the exterior of the buildings. "It seems like Jackson has a skeleton crew on. Is everyone at lunch?"

Steve looked uncomfortable. "I wondered about that too. No, this is his full crew. He said he had a few guys quit to go work at the new RV factory in the next town. More money, different hours. He hasn't replaced them yet. Orders don't seem to be backing up, so maybe business is not as good as it was. I kind of wondered if he really needed me, but he insists that he needs someone to help keep an eye on things."

Why hadn't Jackson said anything about his business being reduced? He had been so supportive of her. Why wouldn't he let her reciprocate? She took the empty chair in the office.

Steve also sat. "Judging by your expression, you didn't know about this. I get the sense a lot of things are riding on this special order. He hasn't said anything officially, but he's pushing the men hard and overseeing this project closely. He's always checking the quality and timeline. I haven't been here long, but I hear the guys talking. They're not complaining, and it's clear they respect him, but even they say he's being overly controlling on this. Just have to wonder why."

Liz shook her head. "I have no idea. Why wouldn't he tell me?"

"My guess is he didn't want to admit to it. The economy is tough right now. Maybe specially made furniture is not as popular as it was." He leaned back in the chair. "But I just came on an hour ago. I can't take lunch right now. I'm sorry."

She smiled, even as her mind was whirling with possible explanations. "No worries. I was just hopeful. It's nice to see you anyway. Come by the inn some night for dinner."

"Sure thing, Mom. Thanks."

She gave him a quick hug, unable to resist the bit of affection, something she hadn't been able to give him for the past several years when he'd been overseas. She'd never get over being able to do it now. She ran a hand through his hair.

"Your hair is starting to grow out."

He grinned ruefully. "Yeah, it's kind of weird not having to rush to get it cut. I might let it get a little longer."

"I like it." She paused. "Your parents would have been so proud of you."

He flushed. "That means a lot, Mom. And you did a pretty good job with me," he grinned. "Thanks."

She hugged him one last time and headed out, leaving him to his job.

Liz decided to head to the clock tower to see how the Sew Welcome and Olde Mansion Inn patch was coming along. Sadie was kneeling in a patch of dirt, barking orders. She wore a hot-pink, broad-brimmed straw hat with a band of multicolored silk flowers to protect her from the sun. From the size of the hat, she could have protected more than one person.

Caitlyn looked up and waved wildly at Liz. "No, Liz, run! Save yourself! It's too late for us, but you can still escape."

Naomi smiled. "Sadie's a brutal taskmaster."

"Less talking, more planting. Oh, it's you, Liz. I don't have you on the schedule until later today." Sadie shot a sharp look at Cailyn and Naomi, who immediately redoubled their efforts by plopping yellow flowers into a series of holes.

"This is looking great, Sadie. The grass makes a pretty green outline for the quilt design."

Sadie straightened and arched her back in a stretch. "Opal and George did a good job laying it out. We're a little behind some of the others, but we'll be okay as long as we stick to the schedule."

"I'm just killing time before I meet with my lawyer. Nancy Redfield is trying to block me from doing any work in that third-floor closet."

Sadie narrowed her eyes and planted her fists on her hips. "I told you she was trouble. What is her problem? You already told her she could have the boxes. Don't say I didn't warn you."

Liz sighed. "Yes, you did. Next time, I'll listen. But Bert said something that got me thinking. Nancy seems more concerned about the idea of a secret room, rather than the boxes. Bert said there was a rumor that Iris Clausen had hidden some kind of treasure or valuables somewhere in the inn. Do you know anything about that?"

"Are you saying I'm old so I must know something?" Sadie replied archly.

"Well, you are," Caitlyn retorted, smiling.

"Then you should show a little respect for your elders, shouldn't you? Get to it, girl. Those flowers aren't going to plant themselves." Sadie turned back to Liz. "I know the rumors. Iris was eccentric and had a lot of money. Or people thought she did, anyway. If any valuables were left, Nancy sold them off years ago. She likes money and fine things." Sadie turned and narrowed her gaze at Caitlyn and Naomi, who had stopped and were listening to the conversation with great interest. "Hey, this isn't television. No commercial breaks, no entertainment. Back to work."

Liz laughed. "Thanks, Sadie. I'll get out of your hair and stop distracting your help."

"Traitor," Caitlyn grumbled.

Liz looked over at the clock tower entrance and saw two figures near the door—Melissa Patton and Pete McConnell. "I'll see you for my shift. Thank you, ladies, for doing such a beautiful job."

She headed over to Melissa and Pete, who immediately stopped talking as soon as they saw her. "I'm so glad you two have met, considering you both have interest in the history of the town."

Pete shuffled his feet. "I had never seen the clock tower, and my grandfather talked about it a lot. I thought it would be fun to check it out."

Melissa frowned. "He was wandering about the inside. I warned him that it needs renovation and we have not fully assessed the safety of every area yet."

"I didn't think it was structurally unsafe, just needed some spiffing up. Are you finding something different?" Liz asked.

Melissa flushed. "No, but we haven't finished our analysis yet. I was just asking Pete for his stories from his grandfather about the tower. I'd love to gather some local anecdotes to add some color to my report."

"And I'd love to hear them."

Melissa smiled, as if excited to share her knowledge. "Well, Iris Clausen, the only daughter of Ralph Clausen, commissioned the clock tower in her father's honor. Ralph collected watches and clocks from all over the world, and she asked to have this one built to replicate a clock tower from her father's hometown in Bern, Switzerland. He was alive when it was built, and they spent time here together before he passed on. According to the stories, she continued to come here to feel close to him, spending time in this garden, until her death."

Liz was enchanted by the story. "What a beautiful memorial to her father."

"The architect, Charles Lawrence, took some liberties with the glockenspiel. Instead of displaying figures in traditional Swiss dress like one would expect, this glockenspiel is unique in that it features Amish characters, in homage to the surrounding community. But the mechanism doesn't seem to be working this morning. I was headed up there to figure out why they didn't come out on the last hour when the doors opened up, like it's supposed to. It might be the gears."

"I didn't know you could fix clocks too," Liz said.

Melissa laughed. "I can't, but I can probably tell if something is corroded or locked up or blocked somehow."

"I love the Amish figures and the tower. It's a real draw to the center of town. That's why several of the local businesses adopt plots of the land here and plant gardens."

Pete looked around. "My grandfather did mention the glockenspiel and a couple of rooms inside the tower, but nothing about these elaborate flower designs."

"The quilt gardens are relatively recent, from the past several years, I think. But I didn't know there were rooms in the tower. I never saw any, although I had a brief tour once." Liz said.

Melissa shook her head. "There are no actual rooms on the plans for the tower, only the spaces for the mechanisms. Perhaps that's what your grandfather meant."

"He said *rooms*," Pete insisted. "I don't know where but they were there. I don't think I misunderstood, though I guess it's possible."

Jim Redfield walked out of the tower at that moment and stopped abruptly. "I didn't expect to see you all here."

Melissa frowned, an expression Liz was beginning to understand was her being possessive about the clock tower. "The tower is supposed to be closed to visitors today while we assess it for renovations and for safety."

He smiled. "Well, my ancestor commissioned it, so I have some leeway when I want to visit it."

Liz cocked her head. "The town of Pleasant Creek owns the clock tower, I believe. And anyway, isn't Nancy the one related to Iris Clausen?"

He flushed. "Well, I helped take care of the woman for years. Believe me, I paid my dues. If you'll excuse me, I see an old friend and would like to catch up."

He lifted a hand in a wave and hurried down the brick path. *Years?* Bert had said Jim and Nancy had lived with Iris for a couple of years, so she supposed he was technically right, but his words were insensitive just the same. Liz glanced at her watch. "Oh my, now I'm running late. I'll catch up with you back at the inn, Melissa."

She hurried down the path after Jim toward her lawyer's office. When she arrived, a few minutes later, she froze. In the shadows between the office and the building next door, figures were talking in voices too low for Liz to make out. It was Jim Redfield and Kent McInerney. As if sensing her presence, they stopped talking and looked over at her. Not knowing what else to do, she raised her hand in a wave. But they just scuttled around the side of the building out of sight. She shook her head and went inside, hoping for good news.

———— ///////////////////////////////// ————

Later that afternoon, Liz changed into gardening clothes and walked back to the clock tower to report for her shift of flower planting. Sadie and Mary Ann, who was also working there, having closed Sew Welcome a bit early, gratefully accepted the jug of iced tea and plastic cups that Liz brought. They all took a break on a park bench to discuss the drama at the inn that morning. Then Liz updated them on the meeting with her lawyer.

"So, at least I know Nancy's threat of legal action has no weight, although she could make things difficult. I'd be able to force her to take her demands to court, which would cost both of us money in legal fees, and she'd almost certainly lose. I already offered her the boxes, which I didn't have to do because legally they're mine. And she has no say at all about the room."

"I can't stand her, never could. That's why I'm staying away from the inn," Sadie said, a slight growl to her voice.

"You're staying away because you're overseeing the planting," Mary Ann reminded her.

"All right, so it has a dual purpose, for which Nancy should be grateful." Sadie adjusted her enormous gardening hat, then poured herself a fresh cup of iced tea.

Liz smiled at her friend. "I just want this over with as soon as possible. Now, I need to find Nancy and break this news to her. When

I got back to the inn, the place was empty except for Sarah, who said no one had been there all day. She was able to get her work done quickly without interruption."

"Avoidance. Works for me," Sadie said matter-of-factly.

Mary Ann grinned. "And I'm grateful that you're practicing that while the Redfields are in town. Stay away until they leave again, please. I'll handle the shop."

Sadie snorted. "I remember talk about them when they moved here to help take care of Iris Clausen. Iris was a nice old lady, just a bit eccentric. But once the Redfields came, things were different. Iris never got out of the house anymore. She used to come here every day to be close to her father. She had a garden plot of her own for him, you know. She loved it here. But they stopped her from coming the last year or so of her life."

"Why would they do that? Was she having trouble getting around?"

"She needed a walker or maybe a wheelchair. She had a man to help her, if I recall, and he'd been with her a long time before they came. But they cut everyone out of her life, except that man. He had been a trusted family friend, but they turned him into a servant, increased his duties and asked him to do more and more even though neither of them was working at the time. Why he stayed on I'll never know. After Iris died, I believe he left town."

"And they converted the house into a bed-and breakfast right after that, I guess with whatever money Iris left them. They never did all that well with the business—their personalities were nothing like yours, Liz." Mary Ann smiled at her.

Sadie rolled her eyes. "The Redfields were terrible at innkeeping because they thought they were better than their guests. Like they were high society. But you know Pleasant Creek. We don't have high society here, nor do our tourists want that."

"So that's why they rented us space for so long for the Sew Welcome Shop," Mary Ann said. "They needed our rental income and the occasional tourist who came to stay just because our store was located right in the building. The arrangement worked until things got ugly with their divorce and their constant arguments were driving our customers away. At that point, Sadie and I decided to take a break from our business. It wasn't like we were making any money at that point."

This was much more information than Sadie and Mary Ann had ever told her about what happened before they appeared on her doorstep expecting to move back in when she'd first bought the inn. It hadn't seemed important before, but now she was grateful to understand.

"And then you came along, Liz, and now everything is perfect," Sadie declared.

Unless Kent has his way.

But no. Whatever her neighbors decided about selling, Liz would never go along with it. "No wonder no one seems to like them." Liz took a long sip of her drink.

"Well, Jim had a few more friends than Nancy," Sadie said. "Nancy treated him horribly, always yelling at him and putting him down. But we were all surprised that he was the one who asked for the divorce. Wouldn't have thought he'd have the backbone for it."

Liz grinned ruefully. "Well, he's grown one since he left her, because he's standing up to her just fine now."

Sadie laughed. "I bet she hates that. Well, enough chitchat. Back to work."

An hour into the planting, Liz glanced up to see Melissa and Kent walking out of the clock tower. She hadn't noticed them go in. They paused by the plot where Liz was working and she stood, grateful for the respite, then dusted her gloved hands together. Kent nodded to her.

"The garden is looking nice. I like the theme," he said.

"Thank you. I heard you were doing the renovations on the tower," Liz said.

"I do more than just build condos, you know. Have you thought any more about my offer?" Kent asked.

"I have, and my answer is still no."

Kent sighed and shook his head. "You do understand how much good we could do for Pleasant Creek with that piece of property, don't you?"

"The Olde Mansion Inn is not for sale, and it won't be as long as I am able to run it. It's a part of Pleasant Creek's history, like this clock tower."

Melissa approached and cocked her head. "What's this about a sale? Are you selling the inn?"

"Absolutely not. But Kent would like me to so he can tear it down and build a new development."

Melissa looked scandalized. "You can't do that. That inn should be on the national registry."

Kent snorted. "Doubtful. It's not that interesting. Even this clock tower is barely history, no matter who the architect was." He turned to Liz. "Let me know when you change your mind. If you think about it as businesswoman and not a silly, emotional female, I think you'll see my offer is the better choice."

He walked away without looking back. Liz glared at his retreating form while Sadie tested the weight of a clod of dirt in her hand. "I could hit him with this. It wouldn't hurt him too bad."

Liz couldn't help a grin as Mary Ann said, "As satisfying as that would be, you probably shouldn't."

She shrugged. "I suppose not. But it would feel good."

Liz turned to Melissa. "Did you figure out what was wrong with the glockenspiel?"

Melissa shook her head. "No, the gears all seem fine. We did move a stick that had fallen in there, so maybe that was it, although Kent didn't think that was the problem. We'll see in the next couple of minutes."

While they waited, Liz offered a cup of iced tea to Melissa, who gratefully accepted.

On the hour, the clock tower chimed and the little door opened, the Amish figures emerging on their platform, high above where the women were standing. Melissa heaved a sigh of relief. "So it was the stick after all."

Liz smiled as the clock tower music played and the chimes counted out the hours. Suddenly, something fell.

Liz ran toward the tower, her stomach clenching, followed by Melissa and Sadie. A body lay on the ground at the base of the structure. It wasn't one of the inanimate Amish figures.

Nancy Redfield was dead.

7

Liz sat on the bench with Sadie and Mary Ann, trying to blot the image of Nancy's body from her mind.

Melissa sat on another bench across the walkway, her face pale with shock. She nodded as Stan Houghton, chief of the Pleasant Creek Police Department, asked her several quiet questions. Melissa rubbed her hands up and down her arms, hugging herself, even though the afternoon sun was warm enough to go without a jacket.

Finally, he stood and walked the few steps across the stone walkway to Liz. "Not what you expected when you worked on the garden today, was it?"

"Not exactly," Liz replied ruefully. "What happened to her?"

"We're not sure. It could have been an accident, though we don't know what she was doing up there. She appears to have hit her head, fallen, and gotten wedged between the figures. Then a loose piece of wood fell into the works—or was placed there—jamming them. Melissa and Kent had been fiddling with the gears and pulled out the stick, which got it moving again."

"How did they miss seeing her body?"

Stan shrugged. "They never checked the figures themselves, only the mechanisms, which are on a different level. Can I speak to you privately, Liz?"

She nodded and followed him to another bench. He asked her for a rundown of everyone she'd seen in and around the park that day, which she gave.

"Know of anyone who might have had a problem with Nancy recently?" he asked.

"Honestly? Just about everyone, including me," Liz replied. "She came back to town to look at some boxes I found in a storage closet, and she proceeded to try to take legal action to prevent me from accessing the room at all, not just the boxes. And she antagonized Melissa, Jim, and Sadie, as well as some others I'm sure."

He grimaced. "Yes, I am aware of the feud between her and Sadie. And Melissa did mention that they argued yesterday, but she didn't seem too troubled by it. What was Jim's reaction to her?"

Liz paused, considering the question. She wanted to be careful, knowing the spouse—or in this case, ex-spouse—was always the top suspect. But there was certainly no love lost between the Redfields.

"He arrived unexpectedly the same day she did. He said a friend told him she was coming back to town, and he told her she owed him half of everything per the terms of their divorce." She looked up at Stan. "The boxes aren't that big a deal. I opened one of them to see what they were. They appeared to be just old pictures and random stuff. Nothing valuable."

He shrugged. "One man's treasure, I suppose. But they had a bitter divorce and a rocky marriage so I'm not surprised that Jim showed up, if only to irritate Nancy. Who knew she was coming here?"

"Mary Ann and Sadie knew, but I'm not sure who else. But still, I got the impression Nancy was less concerned about the boxes than the closet—or what's on the other side of the closet wall. We think there might be a sealed-off room. But what, if anything, is in it is anyone's guess."

Stan looked surprised. "A secret room, eh?" He made a few notes. "Nancy was always a bit difficult. Did she and Jim argue over anything else?"

"No, not that I know of. Everything seemed fine."

"Except with you and the boxes and the room." Stan raised an eyebrow.

Liz wrinkled her nose. "Yeah, I guess that's the main issue here."

"Well, Liz, you know I have to ask. Where have you been since you saw Nancy at the inn this morning?"

"I went to Cross Furniture and saw Steve, then I came here and chatted with Sadie, Caitlyn, and Naomi. I then went to my lawyer's office to review that letter that Nancy gave me from her lawyer. She had no legal standing, which I figured was the case, so I wasn't worried. Then I went back to the inn to change, and I came back here to work in the garden."

He thumbed a few notes into his phone then stood. "Thanks, Liz. Seems like half the town has been in and out of here today, so I have quite a few interviews to do. If I have any more questions, I'll let you know. And if you think of anything, you know where to find me."

"Thanks, Stan."

Stan left for his next interview and Liz sighed. Stan's question brought up one for her. Where was Jim, and who was going to tell him? Even if they were divorced, they must have loved each other once.

Before she could formulate a plan, she saw Jackson striding across the square and she waved to him. He immediately came over to her and wrapped her in a comforting hug. "I just heard the news and came right over. Is Nancy Redfield really dead?"

Liz nodded. "They're not sure what happened. It could have been an accident."

"I can't believe it. I mean, we just saw her this morning. They don't think you had anything to do with it, do they?" He raised an eyebrow.

"Well, we did have a legal dispute, didn't we? But no, my alibi is pretty solid. In fact, I went to the shop to see you and Steve, but you weren't there. I thought you were headed to work after you were at the inn this morning. Where did you go?"

He glanced away. "Nowhere important. I had to go into the city to talk to the bank about a loan. Nothing important."

Liz's mind immediately flashed to the empty workstations and Steve's words about several workers leaving for the RV factory in the next town. Why would he go to an out-of-town bank unless he wanted to keep bad news from circulating in Pleasant Creek? The ramifications were distressing, but she had to know.

She laid a hand on Jackson's arm, turning his attention back to her. "Jackson, is everything okay with your business?"

He gave her a smile. "Of course. It's just a short-term loan, a common practice for bigger orders like this special one I was telling you about. Once we complete the project and get paid by the client, the loan will be paid off."

"You'd tell me if anything was wrong, wouldn't you? I want to be there for you, the way you're always there for me. You're not alone, Jackson."

He gave her a one-armed hug. "I know, Liz. And trust me, I would tell you if I needed to. But everything is just fine. We still on for dinner?"

"Sure," she said. "Looking forward to it."

"Great." He stood. "I have to head back. Stay out of the investigation, okay?"

"I'm sure Nancy just fell. I'll stay out of it as much as I can."

He gave her a fond but skeptical look and headed off. She intended to keep her promise, once she talked to Jim and made sure he was okay.

Liz watched Jackson walk toward the town hall. Just beyond him, Jim was racing down the sidewalk, eyes wide and frantic. She immediately got to her feet and intercepted him.

He stared into her eyes. "I just heard. Is it true? Is Nancy . . . dead?" His voice cracked over the last word.

She laid a hand on his arm. "Yes, Jim. I'm afraid so."

He shook his head, as if denying the facts would make them untrue. She drew him to a concrete bench that was unoccupied. "Let me get Chief Houghton so he can talk to you about what happened."

He gripped her hand as if it were a lifeline. "Don't leave me. I don't know what I'm going to do now." Now that Nancy was dead, some of his animosity toward her seemed to have dissipated. Despite appearances, perhaps he had some residual feelings for the woman. The poor man was clearly in shock.

She glanced over at the bench where Mary Ann and Sadie sat and caught Mary Ann's eye. Liz gestured toward the chief, who was talking to someone closer to the tower. Mary Ann nodded and walked over to get him.

Liz sat down, still holding Jim's hand. "Jim, when did you last talk to Nancy?"

He seemed to rally at the question and gave a short laugh, but it held no amusement. "I wish I could say it was at the inn, but I saw her here after that. I was meeting a couple of friends of mine here. We were hoping to go golfing while I was in town. I decided to take a walk around the tower. I used to bring Iris sometimes when we lived with her. Anyway, Nancy showed up and started yelling at me for getting in her way and ruining everything."

Jim used to bring Iris here? That didn't jibe with what Sadie and Mary Ann had told her. "What do you think Nancy meant by that?"

Jim shrugged. "I have no idea what she meant. Nancy always blamed everyone for her troubles—usually me. She was never happy with anything she had and always felt like people were trying to cheat her out of what she deserved. In fact, she's probably lucky she didn't get what she *really* deserved." His face suddenly crumbled as his words sunk in. "I shouldn't have said that."

"Maybe not." Liz said, glancing up at the chief, who had appeared next to them.

"Jim. It's been a while," Stan said.

Jim struggled to his feet as if shock and grief had stolen his strength. He held out his hand. "What happened to Nancy?"

Stan gestured to the bench, and both men sat. "We're not exactly sure. She died from a blow to the head. She may have fallen, then hit her head, or the other way around. Unfortunately we also have to consider the possibility that she may have been hit on the head deliberately. The investigation and the evidence will have to tell us. But for now, I have a few questions for you."

"I figured you would, since I'm her ex-husband. I'll save you some trouble. Nancy and I had our moments, and we didn't get along very well. We had a rough marriage, mainly because she was a bitter, unhappy woman, and our divorce was not much better. I hadn't seen her since we left Pleasant Creek, nor had I talked to her."

"So why did you come back?"

"Money, of course. I get half of everything she had while we were married. If there was anything in that house that she was entitled to, I wanted half of it, even if it was junk. Honestly, I figured it was probably worth nothing, but I knew it would make her angry if I showed up. After everything I put up with during our marriage, needling her was my right. Besides, I needed to keep her honest. If she had found anything valuable, she would have never shared it with me, never mind our divorce agreement."

"How did you find out about her coming back here?" Liz asked. "Kent McInerney and I have kept in touch. He'd come back to the inn to try to talk to you again and overheard you taking the reservation in another room. So he left and called me. I figured I might as well check it out too."

Kent McInerney. Liz should have known he was involved somehow.

"What do you think is in those boxes, Jim?" Liz asked.

Jim shrugged. "Probably nothing. But I'd appreciate it if you'd let me look through them now just in case. With Nancy gone, I guess they're mine. I'm sure there are no legal means to force you, but I'm hoping you'll let me do it anyway."

She'd have to think about that. As far as she could see, Jim had even less claim on the boxes than Nancy did.

"What about that third-floor room?" Stan asked.

He looked thoughtful. "I admit I'm curious, but I don't know anything about that. Kent is a contractor. He could break the wall down so we can see what's on the other side. I don't think it would be much trouble, and it certainly wouldn't compromise the structure of the building if it was put up after the place was originally built."

"What do you think Nancy thought might be there?" Liz asked, preempting Stan's questioning. Stan frowned, but didn't say anything.

"Nancy had probably run out of the money from the sale of the inn. I think she was hoping to find some valuables she could sell," Jim offered.

"So, Bert's story could be true? There could be missing valuables from Iris Clausen?" Liz asked.

Jim shook his head. "Highly doubtful. Trust me when I say Nancy went over that house with a fine-tooth comb. If money or the potential for money was involved, she'd sniff it out. If it was there, she would have found it."

"But she never found that room," Liz pointed out.

He shook his head. "Neither one of us did. And Nancy might be alive right now if we had."

8

Liz retreated to the inn and made sure Nancy's room was locked and secure, per the chief's instructions, until he could check it out for himself as part of the investigation. Once that was done, she joined Mary Ann and Sadie, who had returned with her, in Sew Welcome. Opal had a routine doctor's appointment, but Caitlyn and Naomi had shown up to circle the wagons and provide support and comfort as they always did. Not for the first time, Liz was grateful to be in Pleasant Creek, to have found a family and people who cared about her. She settled in with a quilt block to relax and unwind from the stress of the past few days.

"I can't quite believe she's gone," Mary Ann said.

Sadie shook her head. "I didn't like her, but I certainly didn't expect her to end up dead." She took a duster to the cutting counter and began to swipe vigorously, even though the surface appeared clean. Sadie, farmer and business owner, was never idle.

"Of course not," Naomi said. "Do they know what happened yet?"

Liz blew out a sigh. "Not for sure. We'll just have to wait." She loaded her needle with stitches the way Sadie had taught her and pulled the thread through the fabric. The rhythmic motion soothed her.

Caitlyn turned to Mary Ann. "If Nancy made things so difficult for you when she owned the inn, why did you continue to lease space from her?"

Mary Ann shrugged fatalistically. "Well, as I told Liz before, it wasn't so bad until the last year or so. By then we'd been here so long it didn't make sense to move."

Sadie waved the duster in the air. "But she constantly made us look bad, like we didn't know what was going on in our own shop. Of course, Nancy also treated the shop as if she owned it and we worked for her."

"Those coupons she offered—why didn't you refuse to honor them? You had the right to do that," Liz said.

Sadie snorted. "We could hardly do that, could we? Those customers would never come back. And Nancy ignored anything that didn't fit into her worldview."

Mary Ann cleared her throat meaningfully.

"What?" Sadie demanded. "You know it's true. I'm sorry she's dead—yes, I truly am. But she wasn't a very nice person, and she took advantage of people. Liz was her latest victim. No, I'm not surprised something happened to her. I just can't imagine who would have done it. She's been gone from Pleasant Creek for a while, and as far as we all knew she'd be leaving again. So why bother to kill her?"

"Sadie, we don't know that she was murdered. It could have been an accident, though what she was doing up in the clock tower I can't imagine," Mary Ann said. Then she grinned. "Besides, you've been known to hold a grudge for years. Why, you and Opal argued over a certain first-place prize in sewing for years. And aren't you still mad at Elwood Draycutt for ruining your doll in second grade?"

Sadie harumphed. "It was my favorite doll. And I'll forgive Elwood when he grovels properly." She laughed with them, then sobered and said, "But seriously, I am sorry for her. She was a pill to many people in town, including her own cousin, Iris, whose house she was living in. But, in my experience, people who are unpleasant are unhappy with themselves and that's sad."

"Enough of this negativity. What's the deal with this Melissa woman who's staying here? She's spending an awful lot of time with Jackson," Naomi said. "They came into the bakery yesterday and today together."

Liz chuckled. "Now don't go reading anything into that. Melissa is a consultant on the tower renovations. Jackson has to work closely with her and oversee the project to ensure it stays on budget and on target. He's also an old friend of her husband's, so they probably have some catching up to do."

"She does seem nice." Naomi took a few stitches on the lap quilt she was working on.

"She is. She's also very passionate about what she does, and Jackson has worked with her before, so he vouches for her skill. We're lucky to have her, I think."

Two customers came into the shop, Susannah Bieler, Liz's neighbor across Jaynes Lake, and Liz's cousin, Miriam Borkholder. Liz stood to greet both women. Miriam gave Liz a warm smile and introduced Susannah, even though Liz knew her from occasional visits to the shop. Susannah was in her fifties, quiet and solemn, but seemed pleasant and friendly at the same time. She fingered a lovely yellow calico—even though she would never sew with anything but solid colors—and began to speak with Mary Ann about a project she was working on. Liz and Miriam chatted a few minutes before Miriam joined Susannah and Mary Ann at the cutting table.

Liz sat back down. "So, I need some advice, ladies. I need a contractor for a renovation on the third floor of the inn. I meant to ask Jackson for a recommendation, but with everything going on, I forgot to ask him. And please don't say Kent McInerney."

Scissors clattered to the floor over at the cutting table, and the women all turned to see Susannah bending over to pick them up.

"Is everything okay?" Mary Ann asked.

Susannah nodded, a slightly nervous look on her face. "It's fine. I just got a little clumsy. Sorry."

Liz exchanged an uneasy glance with Miriam, who shook her

head. "Just tell her, Susannah. She needs to know. No one here will repeat it, I promise you."

Liz stood and walked over to the table. "Susannah, what's wrong? Can I help with anything?"

Susannah stared at Liz, her blue eyes wide and uncertain. She studied Liz for a long moment, then came to a decision. "You've been a good neighbor, friendly and kind. You brought us food and offered to help when my husband got sick last year. It's only fair you should be warned. Kent McInerney wants to buy your land to build it into a housing development for rich people."

Liz nodded. "I know."

"He made my husband an offer to buy our farm, although I'm sure it wasn't as generous as what he'd offer you. He doesn't think much of the Amish, and often tries to overprice his services or pay us less than we deserve. He thinks we're not smart enough to understand the value of things."

Liz nodded. "He offered me a lot of money to buy the Olde Mansion Inn earlier this week."

"Liz!" Sadie said. "Tell us you're not thinking about selling to that skunk!"

Liz shook her head. "Not in a million years. This is my home, my business. Where would I go if I sold it? Besides, what would happen to Sew Welcome?"

Mary Ann quietly cut fabric as the other women gave exclamations of relief and approval. Liz made a mental note to speak with her when no one else was around, to see what was bothering her. Maybe Mary Ann would open up to her.

"Well, Susannah, if there is anything I can do, please let me know. But if I won't sell, and you won't sell, his project just got a lot smaller. If it happens at all."

Susannah looked relieved. "I'm so happy to hear that. We were worried that you would agree, and then we would be forced out. I'll tell my husband about your decision. If you change your mind, will you let us know first so we can be prepared?"

"Of course," Liz said. "But I won't change my mind."

The conversation moved on to other things, and after a bit, Miriam drew Liz to the side. "Thank you for relieving her mind. I told Susannah you would be honest with her and I doubted you would sell, but she has been so worried. I don't know what Kent said to them but I worry that he made threats."

Liz was troubled by Miriam's words. She had gotten the sense that Kent didn't like to be told no, and that he was angry about her refusal. She had wondered if he would turn even less pleasant if she continued to refuse. "Thank you for the heads-up. I'll be careful with him. And please reassure Susannah that I have no intention of selling."

"She thought maybe you'd be marrying Jackson and moving into his house, and closing your business, so you had reason to sell."

Liz was taken aback. "Why would she think that?"

Miriam smiled. "You've been stepping out. It's natural for a couple to eventually marry. He wouldn't want to live in an inn, with his wife serving other people, would he? Jackson seems to make a comfortable living and has a nice home, I believe. He might not want to live in a small apartment here." As if sensing Liz's shock, Miriam laid a hand on Liz's arm. "I'm sorry. It just seemed like the natural next step for both of you. Maybe I was wrong. I'm so sorry."

Liz shook her head, mind still whirling with the idea. "No, Miriam. It's okay. We haven't even discussed marriage. I don't know if we're there yet."

"Oh dear. I've offended you. I'm so sorry. Please, forget I said anything."

"No, Miriam, it's okay. Really."

Liz patted her cousin on the arm and then returned to the group, absently carrying on idle chitchat with the ladies as they packed up their quilts to head home for the evening. Liz was preoccupied with the seed that Miriam had planted in her mind, and as soon as she could, she excused herself to go to the front desk and sort through the day's mail, while her brain turned over the thought of marriage.

Liz wasn't sure how she felt about marriage to Jackson. He was a fine man—the finest she'd ever met—but was that where their relationship was heading? Maybe. The thought wasn't entirely unpalatable, she had to admit.

Miriam had made a good point—if they did marry, where would they live? Would she have to consider giving up this business she had built? She loved what she did now, and was so much happier than she'd ever been as a lawyer. But how could she run a bed-and-breakfast if she lived somewhere else?

She gave herself a mental shake. It was far too soon to be worrying about that. If and when the time came—and that was a big *if*—she and Jackson would deal with the decision together. For now, she needed to forget Miriam had said anything and focus on Nancy and this whole mess. Everything else would work itself out. Eventually.

Sadie poked her head out of the shop. "So this is where you disappeared to. Were we too much for you? It's been a stressful day."

"I'm fine. But how are you doing? I know you had a tumultuous relationship with Nancy, but it still couldn't have been easy for you after knowing her and leasing from her for so long."

Sadie smiled. "Why do you always do that?"

"Do what?"

"Focus on everyone else and not let anyone take care of you?"

Before Liz could answer, Jim Redfield burst through the front door. As soon as he saw them standing by the desk, his face flushed and he stormed up to them. Looking at Sadie, he said, "You! How can you just stand there as if nothing is wrong?"

Sadie looked confused, her brow furrowed and mouth open. "I don't know what you mean, Jim," she said evenly. "I'm so sorry about Nancy. I know we had our differences, but I never wanted anything to happen to her."

He loomed over her. "Don't say anything about her. You hated her and you know it. You and Nancy always fought because you were jealous of her. You also knew she would have made Sew Welcome much more successful than you ever could. She was twice the businesswoman and visionary you are. Instead of learning from her and working with her, you tormented her and made her life miserable."

Sadie stared at him, for once, not on the attack. "Jim, believe me when I tell you I was never jealous of her. If she owned the shop, she would have ruined it. She was too impulsive and spent money unwisely. You know this."

He glared at her. "You were at the tower all day today. Who's to say you didn't slip away and hit her over the head and throw her onto that platform? Just admit it. You killed Nancy! I told the chief that too."

Sadie's face flushed beet red, and her patience seemed to evaporate. "How dare you? How could you even think I would do that? You're awfully specific on the details. Maybe *you* did it."

Jim flinched as if she had struck him, and his face paled. Then his eyes narrowed and his fists clenched, but before he could say or do anything else, Liz pushed herself between them and held up her hands. "Jim, you head up to your room. I can bring you some coffee if you'd like."

With a final narrowed gaze at Sadie, he turned his attention to Liz. "No, thank you. I have dinner plans. But I will go upstairs. I hope

I won't have to be exposed to this woman and her hatred for my wife any longer." He whirled on his heel and stalked to the stairway without a backward glance.

"I had nothing to do with Nancy's death!" Sadie called after his retreating back, but he ignored her. Sadie turned to Liz and Mary Ann, who'd come out of the shop at the commotion. "I may not have liked her, but plenty of people didn't like her. How convenient of him to forget that he disliked her enough to divorce her. I'm going home."

Mary Ann nodded soberly and hugged Sadie. "I know you're innocent, Sadie. But please, watch what you say, okay?"

"You know me."

"That's why I'm asking you to be quiet."

9

The inn was silent after Sadie, Naomi, and Caitlyn left and Mary Ann closed the shop. Melissa and Pete were still out, leaving Mary Ann and Liz alone in the rotunda.

Mary Ann glanced around and gestured toward Liz's quarters. "Could we speak privately?"

Liz nodded and they went inside, closing the door behind them. Once they had settled on the couch, Mary Ann wouldn't meet her gaze, her hands twisting nervously in her lap. Finally, she sighed and looked up.

"I'm worried about Sadie. This whole thing with Nancy is not good. Everyone knows she and Nancy hated each other."

"Was it hate or just mutual dislike?"

"Well, maybe 'hate' is too strong a word. But their arguments could be intense. And a lot of people knew about them."

"I can imagine. And it would only take one person overhearing words said in anger to start spreading rumors and half-truths around Pleasant Creek." Liz had lived in this small town long enough to know how fast gossip could spread.

"And people here have long memories, which are no doubt being sparked by Nancy's death." Mary Ann's normally serene countenance was troubled.

"You said your disagreements had escalated just before Nancy and Jim divorced. Did you mean between Nancy and yourself? Or Sadie?" Liz was fairly sure she knew the answer. Mary Ann was no pushover, but she was a peacemaker, not a combatant.

"They had. Nancy took some of her anger at Jim out on Sadie, and we both know Sadie gives as good as she gets when cornered. I think she would have evicted us, but she needed the money. Neither she nor Jim were ever good innkeepers, no matter what Jim said. Certainly they didn't have the ingenuity to set up theme weekends and specialty gatherings like you've done. The bottom line was she didn't like entertaining strangers in her home, didn't really want to work, and that attitude repelled everyone."

"I can see why she and Sadie wouldn't mesh."

"That's putting it mildly."

Judging by the look on Mary Ann's face, something else was up. "Mary Ann, what aren't you saying?"

Mary Ann sighed. "I may as well spit it out. As I said, I'm worried about Sadie. When I got to the garden today, she wasn't there. And it was a good twenty minutes before she reappeared from the tower. When I asked her what she was doing in there, she said she hadn't been inside in years and wanted to check it out before the restoration changed it." That sounded reasonable, even though Melissa had said no one was supposed to go inside. Still, it hadn't been roped off or anything. "Go on." Liz held her breath, waiting for Mary Ann to continue.

"She didn't tell the chief about it."

Liz's heart sank. "Well, maybe she knew how it sounded and didn't want to expose herself. Or maybe she forgot or didn't think it was important. Would it help if I talked to her? If she needs us, we'll help her. That's what we do for each other."

Mary Ann's shoulders sagged. "She clammed up when I pressed her. I was hoping you'd offer and that you'll have better luck. She could be in real trouble if she doesn't come clean."

Liz hugged her. "I promise you that I'll give it my best shot."

Her friend stood, relief clear on her face. "I knew I could count on you. Thank you so much, Liz. Now, go enjoy your date."

Liz walked her out. Just as she closed the door behind Mary Ann, her phone buzzed with a text message from Jackson.

Sorry. Need rain check. Tomorrow?

Liz replied, *No problem. Take care.*

Trying to stifle her disappointment, she headed for the kitchen. Was there a problem? It wasn't like Jackson to break a date without telling her the reason. Why wouldn't Jackson confide in her about any of his troubles as Mary Ann did? This was why she needed to keep her expectations reasonable about their relationship. Besides, she had enough going on with a murdered guest and now with the added distraction of Sadie. Surely her friend hadn't done anything to Nancy. But Sadie had to come clean with the chief before her omission—or lie, if that's what it was—was exposed.

After a light dinner, Liz drove to Sadie's. The woman was more sensitive than she let on, and she must be upset over the confrontation with Jim. Liz had packed up some lemon squares, hoping the treats might provide a little comfort.

When she arrived at Sadie's farmhouse and made her way up the path to the door, she saw a silhouette in the kitchen window. Sadie sat at the table, staring off into nothingness, a coffee cup on the table in front of her, apparently forgotten. Liz sighed, her heart aching for her friend.

She rapped on the door and Sadie opened it, her cat Dipsy Doodle in her arms. Her expression flashed from apprehension to relief, as if she'd expected someone else. "I thought you had dinner plans."

Liz smiled, trying not to let her disappointment show. "Jackson had something come up so I thought I'd drop by and see how you're doing. I also brought some sustenance." She held up the plate.

Sadie's lips lifted up into a ghost of a smile, but it didn't quite reach her eyes. She put the cat down and he scampered off, maybe because

Buster, Sadie's fox terrier, came trotting in. "Thank you, but I'm not feeling very hungry tonight."

Liz bent down to pet the dog. "You should bring him by to play with Beans."

Sadie stared at her, then laughed, which Liz had been hoping for. "When did Beans start playing? He's much better at lying around. But they did get along pretty well at Beans's birthday party when you first got here. Remember?"

Liz chuckled as Buster stood up against her knee to encourage further attention. "I'll never forget that party." She glanced at the cup on the table. "Do you want that warmed up?"

Sadie chuckled ruefully. "I'll brew a new pot for us. By then I'll probably want one of those lemon squares."

Liz sat at the table, Buster curled up at her feet, and watched Sadie put on the coffee. Sadie switched on the machine, then leaned against the counter. "I argued with Nancy today. Did you know that?"

Liz couldn't betray Mary Ann's confidence, but she didn't want to lie to Sadie either. She said evenly, "What happened?"

"I was so mad that she'd come back to town, creating all sorts of havoc again. Nancy had one talent—making everyone around her crazy. She knew how to find your buttons and push them until you broke. She manipulated everyone around her, kept everyone off balance so they couldn't team up against her. It was amazing that she didn't have more enemies, although she had fewer friends than she thought."

"Who *were* her friends? Who might she have visited when she came back to town? Jim seemed to have people he reconnected with immediately when he got here. According to him he had golf and dinner plans almost before he landed. But Nancy never mentioned anyone."

"Probably because there wasn't anyone. Her old crowd was happy to see the back of her and I doubt she looked anyone up when she came back. No one was with her when I saw her at the tower."

Liz was relieved Sadie had broached the subject of the tower. Now she wouldn't have to find a way to bring it up. "What did you two talk about?"

The coffee finished with a sputter and Sadie filled two mugs, placing one in front of Liz along with sugar and cream. She sat at the table and wrapped her hands around the mug as if to warm them. "We discussed the past. And I admit it was more of an argument than a discussion."

"Oh, Sadie. Did anyone see you?"

"Who knows? That place was more active than an Amish barn raising. It seems like everyone was in and out of the tower today. But no one hung around to chat with us." She leaned back in her chair. "I told her that it was one thing that she'd taken advantage of Mary Ann and me and the shop, but I refused to let her mess things up for you. She would have never let it go, as long as she thought she could get something here."

Liz reached across the table and gripped Sadie's hand. "You are such a good friend to me, Sadie. But Nancy was going to be leaving by the end of the week, once she looked through the boxes. I certainly wasn't going to take down a wall just to satisfy her curiosity. And I was handling the legal side. I appreciate your support, but I don't ever want you to put yourself at risk for me."

Sadie only looked more miserable. Buster whined and nudged her foot with his nose in an effort to console her. "Well, our argument went way beyond that. All the way back to the past. Did you know I consulted an attorney to see if we could sue Nancy for breaking our lease agreement and for lost revenue from those discounts and coupons?"

Liz sat back, surprised, though she supposed she shouldn't have been. "Really? How did she react?"

"She never knew. Mary Ann convinced me to let it go, since the sale of the inn went quickly and you were coming on as owner. And she was right at the time. But when Nancy came back, threatening you with legal action and making demands, I knew I had to confront her."

Liz took a sip of her coffee. "Any idea what she thought might be in the inn?"

Sadie looked thoughtful. "Well, Nancy spent a lot of money—and not on upkeep of the inn, either. It wouldn't surprise me if she ran through the money from the sale of the property and was looking to see if there was anything she had left behind and could claim."

"And she thought there could be something in that third-floor room," Liz mused. "Jim thought that was her motive too."

Sadie nodded. "I think you should get that room opened up and see what's in there."

Liz knew she was right. The only way to put this to rest was to tear down the wall. She took a deep breath and finally asked the question she'd come to ask. "Sadie, I need to know. Did your argument turn physical?"

Sadie's eyes widened. "Absolutely not! We only talked—well, yelled. Then I left. She was alive and fine when I walked away."

"Where did you fight?"

Sadie grimaced. "In the little open area over the figures. You can see the rotating display from above. I think it was open to the public originally, but not anymore, although the stairway to get to it is only chained off. It's easy enough to step over or under. I followed her into the tower and up the stairs. But I left Nancy there alive and unharmed."

"Did you see anyone else at the tower when you left?"

Sadie thought for a moment. "There were quite a few people hanging around. Kent McInerney was looking at the stairway. I remember because he blocked me when I tried to leave, until I finally elbowed him out of the way. I think I saw Melissa around too. Jim must have been there because he told Stan he saw me and overheard us fighting."

This didn't look good for her friend. "I'll do what I can to help, Sadie."

Sadie shook her head. "I'm innocent."

Liz patted her friend's hand. "I know."

After finishing her coffee, Liz went back home. She parked her car, entered through the utility room, and headed for the kitchen, where she checked that everything was ready for tomorrow's breakfast. She had just shut off the overhead light and was about to take a walk around the main floor before settling in for the night when she heard a muffled thud. "That's the library," she said aloud, and headed into the rotunda.

When she got to the library door, she found it closed, which was unusual. She opened it to find Pete McConnell standing over her desk, his hand on the handle of the top drawer.

"May I help you find something?"

Pete jumped and turned, his face flushing. "Yes, I, um, was having trouble getting to sleep and sometimes a good story helps. Sorry if that noise I just made bothered you. I accidentally dropped a book on the hardwood floor."

Liz nodded, though there was no stray book in sight. "Well, as you can see the library has a good-size collection of books. I'm sure you'll find something to interest you. And tomorrow you could check out the bookstore in town. But while you're welcome to enjoy most things here in the inn, my desk is off-limits."

"I wasn't aware of that."

She almost wanted to comment that the drawers were locked,

which ought to be a dead giveaway that no one should be trying to open them, but she kept it to herself. She advanced into the room, and glanced at her normally orderly desk, at the papers that were now slightly askew. The top drawer of her file cabinet was also slightly ajar and she swallowed another sharp remark. She didn't keep any sensitive information in the file cabinet, just brochures and things. But Pete had been taking advantage of her being out to do some snooping. The only question was why?

"If you let me know what you like to read, maybe I could offer some suggestions. Mystery? Suspense? Family drama?" She gave him a sidelong glance.

He shrugged. "I don't know. It really doesn't matter. Anything that would put me to sleep, I suppose."

"So, how is the search for your family's roots going? Find anything?"

He let out a long breath. "I guess I should confess. I was actually looking for information on this house—its history and such. My grandfather said he worked here at one time, a long time ago. I tried the library in town, but they don't have much information considering this is supposedly a historic house and family."

That explanation made sense, though he could simply have asked her for the information. She could sympathize. "I've lived here awhile and don't know much more than I knew when I got here. The Clausen family may have completely died out, now that Nancy is dead, which I assume you heard about." He nodded. "The only child of the man who built the house, Iris, had no children, and the only other relative I know of was Nancy, who was a distant cousin. Bert Worth—you'll find him down at the courthouse most days—and Opal Ringenberg are members of the genealogical society and might be able to help you trace your family." She paused. "What was your grandfather's name?"

"Jones. Joe Jones," Pete stammered.

Liz resisted the urge to roll her eyes. This man was not made for lying, nor was he very good at making up names. "I could introduce you to Bert or Opal tomorrow, if you'd like. Opal often comes to the quilting shop here."

He glanced from side to side and shook his head, backing away. "No, I think I'll be fine. Thank you."

He slipped out of the room, closing the door behind him. Liz shook her head. Pete was certainly a little odd. He didn't seem like the scholarly type. Had he really been looking for historical information?

Or something else?

10

After breakfast, for which no one appeared, Liz sat at her desk in the library, thinking. What had Pete been looking for? Fortunately, she kept all of her important papers and information locked up and in her private quarters. As she pondered, her phone rang.

"Liz, I'm so sorry about last night," Jackson said. "Melissa and I had to meet to talk about Nancy's death and the impact on the renovation timeline."

"Was she okay? It was a pretty horrifying scene to see."

"Well, she's not used to seeing dead bodies. Not that you are." Liz heard Jackson take a deep breath and then blow it out. "I'm botching this entire conversation. I'm so sorry, Liz. Are you okay? I should have checked in on you sooner."

"Jackson, it's fine. I had the Material Girls, and I know you get pulled in a lot of different directions. I'm glad you were able to help Melissa. Is she feeling better today? I didn't hear her come in last night."

"I haven't seen her today. I left her last night after dinner, around eight. I assumed she went back to the inn."

"Well, she didn't come down for breakfast, so she may have left already, or she's sleeping in. I'm not sure. I'll stop by her room later this morning to see if she's okay."

"I appreciate it. How are you doing? Can we reschedule that dinner for tonight?"

Liz smiled. "If you have time. I know how busy you are with the special order and the renovations."

"I have to run to the city again this afternoon, but I should be back in time for a late dinner, around seven?"

"Sounds great." She returned to the kitchen to see Sarah retying the strings of her apron. "Good morning, Liz. I hope you slept well." Her words were innocuous but her face was troubled.

"I'm sure you heard that Nancy Redfield is dead," Liz said, immediately understanding Sarah's distress.

Sarah nodded. "I-I'm worried about Sadie. Is she . . . all right?"

"Sadie is innocent. The police will get to the bottom of this." She hoped she was right about that.

"I know she could never do anything to deliberately harm someone," Sarah said, "but you will help the police, *ja*?"

So far, Liz didn't think she'd been of much help and wasn't quite sure how she could be. But knowing the Amish community's general distrust of the police, Liz tried to reassure her. "I'll do what I can. Do you need some coffee before we start our chores? Let's start by dusting the downstairs and leave the guestrooms for later. I'm not sure who's up and who isn't."

A couple of hours later, they'd finished dusting and straightening the ground-floor rooms and headed upstairs. The yellow crime-scene tape was still across Nancy's door, though, as far as she knew, Stan and his team had finished processing the room yesterday.

Jim came barreling down the hall and stopped in front of them. "You're here to take down this tape, right? I need access to my wife's things."

What was wrong with this man? His ex-wife was dead and he was worried about her belongings? "Jim, I'm sure you know that only the police can take down this tape. And I imagine they'll be by soon to do just that."

"Well her stuff is mine now, and I want it."

Liz's hackles raised. She turned to Sarah, who was busying herself dusting a nearby table. "Sarah, would you check and see if Melissa has left her room? You can start in there and I'll join you." Sarah nodded gratefully. She didn't like conflict anymore than Liz did.

Liz kicked into professional lawyer mode. "You two were divorced, so I don't see how you're entitled to anything. Not that it matters, because no one can go into this room until the Pleasant Creek Police Department allows it."

"It's a good thing I've got a golf date," Jim sputtered. He stormed off to his room and she heard the door slam. She supposed she should cut him some slack. Even though he and Nancy had not been a couple when she died, he must still be grieving in his own way. She just wished he wasn't so . . . entitled.

She and Sarah made quick work of freshening the other guest rooms. Both Pete and Melissa proved to have already left.

Afterward, the two women went downstairs and each ate a slice of the breakfast casserole that Liz's guests hadn't partaken of that morning. Then Sarah went back upstairs to finish her chores.

Liz was just about to pop into Sew Welcome for a chat when the front door opened and Kent McInerney strode in, bold as ever. Just what she needed. She should have gone upstairs with Sarah, and then she might have avoided this man altogether.

"Kent. I didn't expect to see you today."

"Very nice to see you, Liz, although I wish it was under better circumstances."

Liz figured she might as well say it in an effort to save time. "I'm still not interested in selling the inn or its land."

"I'm actually not here to see you or discuss our business deal. In fact, I'm here to see Jim."

"He's gone out, I believe," she said. "How do you two know each other?"

Kent pasted a broad smile on his face, apparently trying to appear charming and nonthreatening but not succeeding. "Jim and I go way back. We played golf often before he moved away. I'm worried about him now. I know he and Nancy were divorced, but it's still a blow. They were married for many years. There's still a connection after all that time."

"Of course," Liz said.

Kent shook his head. "I thought I'd take him out, give him a distraction. But you might want to reconsider my offer. The economy is very tight in town. We're so dependent on tourism. I hear even that Cross Furniture is feeling the pinch."

"I thought you weren't here to discuss business. And I understand what you're saying. You've repeated it enough. But I don't know how to put this any plainer than I already have. I am *not* selling. That's my final answer. Please respect my decision and don't ask again."

Kent straightened, his face flushing.

Before he could speak, Jim came down the stairs, his tread solid and heavy. "Oh. Hi, Kent."

Kent's demeanor changed from angry to sympathetic. "Jim, I am so sorry about Nancy. How are you doing?"

Jim nodded soberly. "I can't believe she's gone. I mean, I know we haven't lived together for a while, but I always knew she was somewhere. Now there's just a hole in my heart, you know?"

Jim was putting on a good show for Kent—or was it for her, after the outburst upstairs?

Kent shot Liz a glare as if she had something to do with his friend's sadness. "Why don't we head out for a cup of coffee before we golf? Take your mind off of things."

"That would be nice." He heaved a heavy sigh and looked around. "I wish we had sold this place to you when we split up. The town would be better off. We would have never come back and Nancy would still be alive."

He turned and walked out the front door. After a meaningful glance at Liz, Kent followed, shutting the door behind him.

"Well, that was interesting." Liz said to herself.

"He could be right," Mary Ann said from the shop entrance, a bolt of fabric in her hands.

Liz jumped then placed a hand on her chest. "I didn't realize you were there. What do you mean? Do you think I'm holding the town back?" Mary Ann couldn't possibly want her to sell to Kent. Could she?

Mary Ann gave a small laugh. "Of course not. One business can't make or break a town, no matter what Kent McInerney says. Could a development with a lot of houses bring in people and taxes? Maybe. But he'd have to get the people to come, and what would the draw be? We're not close enough to the big city for the high-paying jobs, so any expensive homes would probably sit vacant. And our town isn't large or exciting enough for people to be dying to move here. People love to visit and say they'd love to live here, but when push comes to shove, we're just not modern enough for them. And that's all right with me."

Liz grinned. "Me too. Did Kent really make an offer to the Redfields before they left?"

Mary Ann leaned the bolt against the wall and walked over to the desk. "I believe he did, and that Jim wanted to take it, but Nancy refused. I think it was more on principle. Nancy hated Kent and resented the time Jim spent with him. She thought Kent was a little low class. But his offer wasn't high enough anyway. He was way under market value for the place. Kent was hoping no one else would offer and they would be forced to accept him. Then you came along."

Liz whistled. "Well, no wonder he's not thrilled with me."

Mary Ann shrugged. "He doesn't like a lot of people. Have you talked to Jackson about the proposed development? I can't imagine he thinks it's a good idea. I don't know if it's even passed the zoning committee."

"Kent can't get through zoning until he already owns the land. But if the town isn't behind this, why is he pushing so hard?"

"Who knows?" Mary Ann started to turn back to the shop, then paused. "Thanks for going to see Sadie. I talked with her last night and she sounded much better. I know she still feels bad, but she's happy that we believe her."

Liz bit her lower lip, her mind back on the troubling death of Nancy Redfield. "I really can't imagine Sadie hurting anyone. She may sound a bit cranky at times, but she has a heart of gold and would do anything for anyone, even Nancy. But honestly, I don't know who could have killed her."

"What does the chief think?"

"I plan to ask him that when he comes to release Nancy's room. Jim's been pushing me to let him go through it, and I'd like to make sure there's nothing perishable in there too. Stan said he'd be by later this morning."

Mary Ann laid a hand on Liz's arm. "Well, if anyone can figure it out, it will be you. Thank you so much for helping Sadie."

"She's my friend too. And I'm sure Stan doesn't think Sadie is guilty."

"You know we have to consider the possibility that she did it." Stan studied Liz over the rim of his coffee mug later that morning.

Stan and Liz were sitting in the kitchen, enjoying a cup of coffee and some scones. Stan looked tired, as if he had been up most of the night working on the case, which he might very well have been. He scrubbed a hand over his face and took another sip of the coffee.

"I don't understand, Stan. Sadie said when she left Nancy she was fine."

Stan gave a small smile. "And no murder suspect lies. I know Sadie, Liz, and I can't imagine it either, but she's the last person we can confirm who saw Nancy before she died. They had a very tumultuous history, including legal action. Money and anger are powerful motivators."

"Not the last person." When Stan gave her a blank look, Liz folded her arms. "Her murderer was the last person to see her alive. And I don't believe that was Sadie. I just don't buy it, Stan. Could it have been an accident?"

He nodded slowly. "Maybe. I don't know. I'm waiting on the medical examiner's report for more details."

"There were a lot of people in and out of the tower. It could have been anyone."

He broke off a piece of scone and applied a layer of butter. "For a place that was supposed to be closed for renovations, it did see a lot of traffic. I have some more interviews to do, but Sadie is a top suspect right now. And she'll remain one until I find something that proves she couldn't have done it. That's protocol."

"Who else did Nancy see while she was in town?" Liz asked. If Stan needed proof of Sadie's innocence, she would help him find it. Though Sadie had said it was unlikely Nancy had any friends left in Pleasant Creek.

Stan leaned back in his chair. "That's a good question. I can't find anyone she talked to except her lawyer. I hear she was looking to sue you about some contents of a room?"

Liz raised an eyebrow at him. "Is this an interview, Stan?"

"Consider it a follow-up. Did she talk about legal action about some contents of the inn?"

Liz nodded. "Yes, I had contacted her about some boxes I found in a storage room. Technically, I owned them according to the sale agreement, but the contents looked personal and I thought she might want them. I was trying to be nice, and you see where that's gotten us. So, I called her and offered them to her. She wasn't interested until I mentioned that we thought there might be a sealed-off room behind the closet where we found the boxes. Suddenly she decided she wanted to come here."

Stan stood. "Mind if I take a look at that closet?"

"Sure." Liz shrugged and led him upstairs. "My lawyer said she had no legal claim to either the boxes or whatever's in the walled-off space."

Liz unlocked the closet door and Stan stepped inside. She flicked on the light and they glanced around. He gestured to the corner. "Have you started working on the wall already?"

Liz bent over and peered at a small corner where the wallpaper had been peeled away and a hole had been drilled into the wall. A pile of wood dust lay on the floor under the hole. She squatted and tried to look into it, but the hole didn't reach all the way through the wall. "No, I didn't do this or order it to be done. I haven't hired a contractor yet. Kent McInerney is the only one I know of, and he wants to buy the inn, so I'm not keen on using him right now." The boxes, at least, were safely stowed in Liz's quarters where Jackson and Steve had set them right after they discovered them in the closet. She'd seen them, undisturbed, this morning.

Stan nodded. He gestured for her to move out of the way and knelt down to check it out. "Someone is trying to find out what's on the other side. Who might have done it?"

Liz shook her head. "I have no idea. And I'm not sure how he got in, since the door was locked. I'll have to ask one of my guests who is staying up here if he has heard anything."

"Let me know what you find out. But it might be good to break down that wall sooner than later and see what everyone is interested in. It may not mean anything, but then at least you won't have people sneaking in here to treasure-hunt." He sighed. "Well, let's head down to Nancy's room so I can release it."

"Thanks, Stan."

Liz followed Stan down one flight of stairs and headed back to the kitchen while Stan went through Nancy's room. Stan was right about one thing. She had to figure out why that room had been so important to Nancy and now to someone else—assuming it was someone other than Nancy who'd drilled that hole.

11

Liz had just poured herself a glass of cold water after Stan had left when her phone rang. She looked at the display. Tom Martin? Liz frowned. Why was her lawyer calling her? He'd told her Nancy's claim was worthless.

She answered the phone and took her water into the library, walking as she spoke. "Tom, I didn't expect to hear from you. What can I do for you?"

He cleared his throat. "Liz, I'm so sorry. As I promised, I did some further research into the sale documents to ensure I was providing you with the right guidance, and I think I gave you some erroneous information."

"I don't understand, Tom." She sat down at her desk.

"In the original sale documents, there was a clause that any items not specifically listed as part of the sale and found later had to be shared with the Redfields."

Liz narrowed her eyes and tapped a finger against the desk. "I don't understand how we missed that. We never did a complete listing of all of the contents of the inn. Basically, that implies that anything not listed can be claimed by the Redfields at any time."

"Not exactly. We had rooms specified along with their contents. Because the third-floor room is now suspected of having another room behind it, well, that room, supposing it exists, is not specifically named in the sale documents. In fact, the third-floor storage closet was not clearly stated in the sale documents at all."

"Again, how did we miss that?" Liz was stunned. As a former lawyer herself, she should have caught that.

"I'm sorry, Liz. It's a nonstandard clause, and quite honestly I don't remember it. All I can think of is that it was a requirement of the sale, that the Redfields required it in the contract."

Liz sighed. "So, what does this mean now that Nancy's dead?"

"I'll have to do some research on that, and it might depend on her will and who her beneficiary is. But whoever that is, they would have a claim on anything in that room. I'll have to give this some thought before I can recommend the next steps."

"Okay, thanks, Tom. Anything you can do would be appreciated."

She ended the call and swiveled her chair to gaze out the window over the lawn. When had this situation spiraled out of control? It had started with trying to do a nice thing, a gesture of goodwill in an effort to ensure that Nancy had her family's things returned to her.

Guilt prodded her as she thought about Jim Redfield's words. If Liz hadn't called Nancy, the woman would still be in Boca Raton, oblivious and alive. Had Liz caused her death, even if she hadn't murdered her? Just by trying to do the right thing, she'd set into motion these events that had escalated into an untimely death. No matter how nasty she may have been, Nancy hadn't deserved what had happened.

Someone knocked on the doorjamb, and Jim and Kent entered without waiting for her to admit them. Jim looked furious, his brows drawn low and face red.

"Liz, by now, I assume your attorney has informed you of my legal claims here at the inn. I was just on the third floor and I noticed your servant going into that closet. I thought we were very clear that access to that space was to be denied to everyone until we've resolved ownership."

Liz stiffened. "First of all, I don't have a servant. I have a part-time employee who is authorized to use her key and go where she needs to in order to complete her work here. And second, we didn't agree to anything. I am running a business here and I'll decide what happens in my own home."

Jim and Kent glared at her, but Liz refused to back down. Who did these two think they were?

"It's time to tear down that wall and get this cleared up once and for all," Jim demanded. "Kent is here right now, and he and his crew can do the job."

Not in a million years.

She stood and braced her hands on the desk. "No. I will not use Kent to take down the wall—if I decide to do it. I will find a neutral party to do the demolition."

"So, you'll hire your boyfriend?" Jim's voice was snide

"Maybe. Are you paying for it? *I* don't have any pressing need to do work on my house."

Jim looked stricken, but quickly recovered himself.

"As long as I own the Olde Mansion Inn," Liz continued, "I will make the decisions. You abdicated that responsibility when you sold it. You're welcome to sit outside the room until I can get a new lock for the door. You wouldn't happen to know how someone got into that closet, would you?" Neither answered, but she'd bet money it had been one—or both—of them who'd broken in and drilled into the wall. "I have acted in good faith in this entire situation. I would never do anything to interfere in anything that's legally owed to you."

She met both Jim and Kent's gazes evenly.

Finally Jim sighed and seemed to deflate. "Fine, Liz. I believe you mean well. I just want to be sure no one else takes advantage of you." Jim turned to Kent. "Come on, Kent. I have to make funeral arrangements for Nancy, and I could use your support."

With a final glare at Liz, Kent stomped out the door after him.

Liz was still in the library when Sarah came in, looking hesitant. Liz waved her in.

"Can we talk for a moment? The door to the third-floor storage closet isn't locked anymore. It seems to be broken."

Liz nodded. "I'll get a new lock put on it today. For now, use the cleaning supplies from the second floor, okay?"

"People are very interested in that closet," Sarah said. "The young woman and man both asked me about it yesterday."

"Melissa? Pete?" She supposed it was only natural they'd want more information.

"And I saw Kent McInerney up there this morning too. He said he was waiting for Jim and needed to use the bathroom. I told him he could use one of the unoccupied rooms, but he just gave me a nasty look. I don't like him."

Liz turned a sharp look on her. The statement was out of character for her normally mild-mannered employee. "Why not?"

"I know he has been pressuring some of the other Amish to sell their farms, not just around Jaynes Lake. He's trying to push the Bielers out right now, and not even offering them fair price for their land."

"I know about the Bielers. Has he tried anything underhanded to get people to sell?"

Sarah looked uncomfortable. "Nothing we can prove, but some of the Amish are afraid of him and his crew. He doesn't respect our ways. He intentionally passes our *Valgas*, our buggies, too closely and at high speeds to frighten our *Gelus*, our horses. He has no respect except for force and money, neither of which the Amish have."

"Thank you for sharing that, Sarah. I'll make sure the room is secured."

"Let me know how I can help." Sarah smiled and left the room.

So Kent had been snooping upstairs. That was interesting. He would have had the tools to get into the room and figure out what was behind the wall. But why would he care what was in the room? He'd made no secret that he planned to tear down the inn for a housing development. What did he care if there was a secret room or not? Of course, he and Jim were probably working together.

Could it be tied to the rumors of missing valuables? Yet, there appeared to be no way in or out, so whatever was in that room must be intact from the time it was closed up.

The most likely scenario was that the Clausens had split the old nanny's room into two rooms for servant quarters. At some point, when the house didn't require so many servants, the Clausens may have closed it up and the space was forgotten. When the wall came down, she suspected all she'd find would be a thick layer of dust and maybe a couple of spare pieces of furniture.

Liz called Jackson, who promised to bring the materials by later to put a padlock on the door as a temporary measure before they went out.

Jackson was as good as his word and installed a hasp and padlock in short order. They headed out to Pasta Heaven for dinner. He had reserved an intimate table in a small alcove that afforded them a bit of privacy. He pulled out her chair and then slid in across from her.

"I'm so glad we're finally able to do this. I feel like it's been too long since we had some time for just us," Jackson said, a warm smile crossing his face. "I've missed you."

Liz smiled, the tension from the past several days drifting away. "I agree. I know the circumstances have made it difficult for us to coordinate. Did you get your business finished?"

He shook his head. "I don't want to talk about business tonight. Let's talk about something else."

"Like what?" Liz laughed. "What do you think everyone is talking about? Nancy Redfield? The renovations of the tower?"

He sighed. "Let's not talk about Nancy either. As for the tower, it's slow going. Anything historic usually is. We have so many permits and approvals to get through. There's so much red tape to maintain the historic integrity, you know? I understand why it's necessary, but sometimes it's frustrating when you just want to get started. And it's worse right now because it's locked down for the investigation."

Liz laughed. "I can only imagine. And Melissa seems the type to ensure all protocols are followed explicitly."

He grimaced. "Yeah, I should have remembered that when I recommended her for the job. She's definitely the right person for it, but the whole process is a giant pain." He picked up the menu. "Anyway, enough about work. Shall we try the specials or something off the regular menu?"

"I think the specials tonight. What's the damage to the timeline for the renovation? And do you know when we'll be able to get back into the garden?" Liz slathered local homemade honey butter on the fresh bread, hoping to stave off the hunger that had been gnawing at her all afternoon.

Jackson raised an eyebrow at her. "I guess we're talking about Nancy's murder anyway," he said wryly. "The chief said he'll release the crime scene as soon as he can, but tomorrow might be out for working there. He wants to be sure they haven't missed anything before he lets people in." Jackson also reached for some of the bread.

"Will that keep Melissa here longer? Will it affect her other work?"

He shrugged. "She may not stay for the whole project. She does have other work lined up, I'm sure. Why? Do you need her room at the inn?"

Liz shrugged. "Just keeping track of rooms and vacancies. How are things at the furniture company? How is Steve working out?"

Jackson grinned, but Liz thought she detected a few lines of strain. "And I guess we're talking about business too. To be honest, we're a bit lean right now. The RV factory is expanding and hiring, and it's paying a lot more than I can afford to. Not to mention it's hard to find experienced woodworkers these days. It's a dying art, unfortunately, even among the Amish. Since I haven't had as many orders coming in as usual, I decided to not worry about replacing some of the workers for now. But I have the positions posted. If I find qualified workers, I'll hire them."

The bread turned to sawdust in Liz's mouth. "So, this special order is a big deal."

He shrugged. "It's a nice coup for us. It could expand my business and continue to bring in specialized orders. But I still need craftsmen to work the wood. No getting around that."

Liz placed a hand over his. "Is there anything I can do to help?"

He shook his head. "Just listen as you have been. Now, enough of this maudlin talk. Let's talk about anything but death, business, and other people."

The waitress brought their meals and they dug in, laughing and enjoying the rest of the evening. Yet somehow Liz still felt that Jackson was hiding something from her, and she wondered what it was.

12

The next morning Liz decided to head out to the clock tower to work on the garden, now that the chief had released the scene and allowed them to resume the planting. When Liz drove up, she found a lone figure in the Material Girls patch. Sadie wore the same hot-pink broad-brimmed straw hat as before, rolled-up jeans, and a T-shirt. She straightened when she saw Liz get out of her car. Liz waved and pulled out a bag containing fresh fruit and a thermos of iced tea, which she set out on one of the benches. Sadie joined her, gratefully accepting a plastic cup of tea and sitting down with a sigh.

"That hits the spot. The sun is hot today."

"I wasn't sure you'd be here," Liz said.

Sadie shrugged. "I didn't want to come to the shop, but sitting home was not an option. Stan called and said I could come back here to work. It seemed like it would be good therapy."

"I thought the same thing, even though it's not my official shift. What do you need me to do?"

Sadie smiled. "We can get some of the flowers planted around the edge. I'll show you."

They worked quietly for almost an hour, the drone of passing cars, chirping birds, and the occasional buzzing of insects providing a backdrop to the meditative quality of planting. Finally, Liz glanced up and saw Melissa and Jackson standing outside a real estate office across the street on the far side of the garden, heads bent together in conversation. Melissa looked very earnest, as if arguing her point on something, but Jackson's smile was only polite, if a little distant. Then Melissa came across the street through the garden, walking right past Sadie and Liz without acknowledging them, seemingly lost in thought. Liz went back to work.

A couple of minutes later, a shadow fell across the garden plot. Liz looked up to see Jackson standing there, a broad smile on his face. She glanced at Sadie, who continued to work, but Liz had no doubt she was listening to every word.

"I love the way this is turning out," said Jackson. "Great idea, Liz."

Liz straightened, groaning when her muscles protested the movement. "Thanks, but I'm just muscle here. I can't take credit for the design."

"Well, either way, it looks great." Then his brow creased in concern. "Do you need me to talk with Jim or Kent, to settle them down?"

Liz grimaced. As much as she'd love to have Jackson use his position as mayor to get Kent to back off, there wasn't anything he could actually do. She shook her head. "No, I can handle it. We should be all set soon. Our lawyers are looking into it. There's some kind of clause built into the sale agreement that may allow Jim rights to that room, so we'll need to open it sooner rather than later. But first, my lawyer is still looking into the legalities. Hopefully, within the next couple of days. Could you help with the demolition? I don't want Kent anywhere near it."

"Absolutely. Anything you need, let me know."

Liz grinned. "Thanks, Jackson. You've been so helpful."

"Anytime." He gave her a quick kiss before striding away.

She watched him leave, trying to ignore Sadie's broad grin. Finally, she rolled her eyes at her friend. "Shut up, Sadie."

"I didn't say a word."

But Sadie made kissing noises, and as she worked on her section of the flower garden, Liz couldn't help a smile from forming. She continued working on the purple section of the quilt, feeling oddly satisfied.

An hour later, two of the purple sections of quilt were complete, more than Liz had anticipated. Opal had shown up, so the work had gone faster. When they took a break, Bert Worth stopped by, with a small group of people following behind him, and complimented them on the garden.

"This is one of the garden plots that our businesses work on, donating their time and money to make the clock tower grounds look beautiful," Bert explained to the group. "An added benefit is that the garden is on the Quilt and Garden Tour for the state. Sadie is one of the sponsors for this spot as a co-owner of Sew Welcome, a quilt shop located in the Olde Mansion Inn. Liz Eckardt is the other sponsor and the owner of the same inn."

Sadie straightened and smiled at their visitors. "Hi, Bert. Who are your friends?"

"I'm giving a tour of the clock tower to a few tourists, though we can't see the whole thing due to the renovations." He studiously avoided mentioning the recent murder. "Could you tell us about the inspiration for your plot?"

"Sure. All the plots here are based on a quilt design in order to be included in the Quilt and Garden Tour Bert mentioned. This one is the Indiana Star quilt block. We're keeping it simple, using turfgrass as our structuring element to represent seams, then petunias and celosias to fill in as the 'fabric.' It's a lot of work, but we're happy to do our part to make Pleasant Creek, well, pleasant."

A few of the tourists laughed, and Bert nodded enthusiastically. "The Clausen family, who commissioned the clock tower, loved the town and loved flowers. So we do this to honor them. We'll take a five-minute break before we get started. Feel free to walk around and check out the gardens, which, as you can see, are in various stages of completion."

Liz shaded her eyes and scanned the five or six people who broke off from Bert's group. Pete McConnell was in the small group, near the back.

"Hey, Sadie, can you and Opal handle things here for a bit? I'd like to tour the clock tower."

"Go ahead," Sadie told her. "We can take care of this, at least until you get back."

Liz joined Bert. "Would I be able to join your tour? Since I moved here, I've never managed to make time to take it."

"Of course. I've done a bit more research and we've learned so much with the renovations, I've updated the tour. Please join us."

The group reassembled and they headed for the front of the tower. Glancing up, Liz noticed it was just before the hour.

"Our tower chimes every hour and we also have a set of figurines that come out on a track every three hours during the day. Iris Clausen commissioned the tower to be built in honor of her father, Ralph, who loved clocks. For years, she and Ralph came here every day. Once he passed, she continued to visit without fail to hear the clocks chime and to see the figures representing Amish culture. Ms. Clausen died without any direct descendants, and she left her valuable historic possessions to the state historical society."

Three o'clock chimed, and the figures—a man and woman wearing traditional Amish dress—rolled out on schedule. Once they finished, Bert herded his charges inside. "Let's see how this works. We're lucky. The tower is supposed to be closed right now, but I got special permission to bring you all along today."

He escorted them upstairs. Liz maneuvered until she was

standing near Pete. "Did you have any luck talking with Bert about your family?"

Pete nodded. "We've talked a bit, but I have not been able to find my grandfather or his family. I think everyone has passed now, as I had suspected. There is nothing in the record about them though, so maybe his name is incorrect."

Liz nodded, then thought of her own mother. "Could he have been Amish and changed his name when he left the community?"

Pete shook his head vehemently. "No, he didn't." Then his eyes widened, as if he hadn't planned on saying that.

At that moment, they had to climb a set of stairs, then a steep, narrow set of stairs to get to the mechanical area, so the conversation was cut short. When they entered the mechanical room where the gears for the clock were housed, the noise from the clock and Bert shouting to be heard over it also prevented further discussion. Pete slid away, closer to Bert.

Bert explained that this was a mechanical clock which had to be wound three times a week, similar to other clock towers such as Big Ben in London. Many clock towers operated simply by pendulums, but this one was more complicated.

The mechanism looked like a wagon and a series of gears, and Bert explained it was a three-train flatbed clock mechanism, meaning there were three distinct sections to keep the time and the bells working.

He gestured to the first section. "This governs when the bell chimes. We disabled this section because, many years ago, the town decided we didn't want chimes every quarter hour, just a bell on the hour. The second section controls the clock and dial, keeping the time. And the last section rings the big bell."

Pete raised his hand. "Where are the figures?"

Bert smiled. "I'm glad you asked. They are housed below us and work on a set of gears, emerging when the clock chimes. I can't bring you down to show them as we had a little . . . incident the other day and that area is still closed off to the public. But the figures themselves were carved especially for this tower."

"Does this tower serve any other purpose? I mean, it's just standing here and keeps time? Seems like a waste of space to me," one of the other tourists said.

"Not exactly," Bert replied. "There has always been a rumor that there was a secret room in the tower where Iris and her father came every day to have tea. Once he passed, and up until the last couple of years of her life, Iris came every day to visit her father's grave in the cemetery, then here to the clock tower."

Pete visibly perked up. "A secret room? My grandfather mentioned that to me. Where is it?"

Liz's attention was also piqued. Secret rooms seemed to be a common theme with the Clausen family. She was eager to hear the answer.

Bert shrugged. "If I knew, I'd tell you. It's an attractive idea, but we can't confirm it. It's not on any plans for the tower and, since we're in the process of renovating it, we've been looking. The only thing we know is that Iris came here most every day, and she had to sit somewhere, especially in bad weather. Somehow, I doubt she came all the way up here, especially when she got older and had trouble getting around."

The group peered around the small space as if trying to spot a trapdoor or secret entrance. At least, that's what Liz was doing.

"It could have been sealed though, right?" Pete suggested.

Bert, who had started to usher people down the stairs out of the room, paused. "I suppose so, but we've seen no evidence of that."

Pete looked disappointed and stood over by the gears. The people started filing down the stairs, but Pete did a small circuit of the room, studying the walls closely while Liz studied him. While Bert was occupied, she sidled over to Pete. "It's an intriguing story, isn't it?"

"It is."

"You said your grandfather told you about it?"

He shrugged. "He did. Wouldn't it be something if it turns out to be true? We should keep up with the group." He walked away to the stairs.

Liz followed him slowly. Who was this man's grandfather? Was he connected to the Clausen family? He'd said his family names were Jones and Bieler. Liz was pretty sure he was holding back information.

The tour ended and the people scattered, most to walk the gardens, then stroll off toward the downtown shops. Pete lingered inside the building, no doubt looking for the secret room. Liz decided to talk to Bert in private and find out how much he really knew. She was betting it was more than he was supposed to tell tour groups. It made sense. The town certainly wouldn't want people coming back after hours and poking around.

She pulled him aside. "Hey, Bert, got a minute?"

"After a clock tower tour?" He laughed at his own joke. "Of course."

They went outside and sat on a bench in the warm sunlight. Sadie joined them, taking a much-needed break from planting.

"Bert, what do you really know about a secret room in the tower?" Liz asked.

He wrinkled his nose. "I had forgotten about it, to be honest. I went back and did a little digging after the murder, but I didn't find anything substantial. All I know is that Iris Clausen and her father used to come here to see the clock every day. Once he died, she kept up the tradition."

Sadie nodded, her face taking on the faraway look of a person deep in memory. "I remember her doing that. She had a chauffeur or helper who used to drive her here every day. A man who carried a picnic basket. They always went inside, so there had to be a place they sat."

"Could they have gone to the gear room or the figurine room?" Liz asked.

Sadie shook her head. "Doubtful, at least toward the end. Iris used a cane and had trouble getting around. Her companion was also older and couldn't have helped her up the stairs. I remember hearing rumors about a special room. The tower wasn't open to the public like it is now. She was very protective of it, viewed it as an extension of the Clausen family I think, even though she'd given it to the town and the town owns it. She was eccentric. Why are you eccentric when you're rich and just weird when you're not?"

"Who was her companion? Do you remember his name?" Liz asked.

Bert shook his head. "I vaguely recall him. I think he left town right after her death. The Redfields didn't want him around." He and Sadie exchanged glances. "You know, there aren't a lot of people around who might remember Iris in her younger years. Althea Mitchell from the genealogical society is at a conference until next week. But you might check in with Betty Hulbert, Curtis Angly, and Colonel Burns. They may remember more. They hang out at the senior center and love to talk. I told that nice man staying with you about Althea, but I didn't think to mention the rest of them."

"Of course! I should have thought of them. I'll let Pete know too. Maybe they knew his grandfather. Did he tell you his grandfather's name, Bert?"

Bert frowned. "He said he thought it was Bieler, but not related to your neighbors. Wouldn't he know his own grandfather's name?"

Interesting. Why was he giving two different names? Well, the man did have two grandfathers, she supposed. "You would think. Anyway, thanks for the tip. I'll try to catch those folks at the center."

"It's bingo day. I'm sure they'll be there."

13

Liz stopped back at the inn and cleaned up before heading over to the senior center, hoping to catch the three retirees just as bingo ended. She found them playing a game of cards in the sitting room. When Liz asked to join them, they gratefully accepted and offered her a cup of coffee.

She settled in her chair and explained why she was there. The three seniors exchanged pensive glances. Liz let the silence drag on for a few moments to allow them time to refresh their memories on the Clausen family. Finally, the colonel cleared his throat.

"Well, my father was quite friendly with old man Clausen so I knew the daughter. But I wasn't really in their social circle so I never spent a lot of time with them. Betty, you knew Iris a bit better, didn't you?"

Betty slowly nodded. "I volunteered at the church with her, but she was older and we weren't friends. I don't know who *was* friends with her. She and her family kept to themselves, you know? They were in a higher social stratum than almost everyone in Pleasant Creek—or thought they were. I could never figure out why they settled here."

Curtis agreed. "Very true. But perhaps they liked Pleasant Creek for the same reasons we do—it's a lovely, usually friendly small town. But they did stick to themselves, and old Ralph Clausen traveled some for business. They had a couple of employees, but even they stuck to themselves. Iris had a close one in particular. Connelly or McConnell. Something like that."

Liz froze. "McConnell? He worked for Iris?"

"Yes, he was a jack-of-all-trades. He did everything for Iris, and I think the Redfields took advantage of him while they were there. But he was unusually dedicated to Iris until her death. Before the Redfields came to stay, he drove her every day to the tower and sat with her while she had tea after her father passed on. But the Redfields soon stopped her trips to the tower when they came to live with her."

"Did you know this McConnell? I have a Pete McConnell staying with me. He's looking for his relatives, but he says his grandfather's last name was Jones."

The colonel nodded. "I suppose that's possible, but I knew Michael McConnell. They might not necessarily be related. Michael was utterly devoted to the Clausen family, Iris in particular. I think he fancied himself in love with her. Not that he would have acted on it. He knew the score. Ralph Clausen would have never let Iris marry the son of a servant. Michael went to war in World War II. Clausen employed his parents as his cook and chauffeur, then him as a jack-of-all-trades after the war."

"Whatever happened to him?"

The three people looked at each other. Finally, Curtis shrugged. "I have no idea. After Iris died, he left town. The Redfields weren't going to keep him on, at least not in a paying position. I always figured Iris would have left him something in her will, but I wouldn't put it past those Redfields—especially the wife—to find some way to keep the money. Never saw him again. He's probably passed on by now."

"Did he have a family, a wife or anything?"

They all shook their heads, and Betty answered. "As far as I know, no family. Iris was his whole life. Bit of an odd duck. But they all were in that house."

"Why didn't Iris ever marry? It seems odd that she would remain single as an only daughter and a member of that generation."

Betty smiled. "She was unusual in that regard. I think her father indulged her. Her mother died when she was very young. In fact, I don't remember her mother at all. They often traveled for her father's business when Iris was younger. Anyway, Iris usually went with him on his trips when he was still working. But she always came back. Only once did she stay here without him, that I know of. One winter while he went to Europe before World War II, I think. Maybe it was too dangerous. I only remember because we tried to invite her to some of the town events and she refused, saying she couldn't. I had always thought it was her father keeping her from making friends. After that, I wondered if maybe she was merely shy. She didn't seem unfriendly when in town. So who knows?"

"Do you know anything about a secret room in the clock tower?"

"Ahh, the tea room. Yes, Iris had a special room built in the tower where she and her father had tea every day at three. She continued the tradition after his death," Betty said.

"So, it existed? No one has been able to confirm it. Do you know where it was?" Excitement shivered up Liz's back.

But Betty shook her head. "I was so busy with my own family, and no one was really allowed in the tower until after Iris's death. I only know she went there every day. But since she was older when she was going, I think it would have to be on the lower floor. Her father had arthritic knees, so he couldn't do too many stairs either."

Liz nodded, her mind spinning. "Thank you so much for your time. I'll head to the library and see if I can find any more information and share this with Bert too. Do you mind if I send my guest to you to ask about his grandfather? I think he might be related to Michael McConnell, even if he won't admit it to me."

"Of course, Liz. We'd be happy to talk to him. I knew Michael somewhat and would love to hear about how he made out after he left Pleasant Creek," the colonel said.

Liz stood. "Excellent. You've all been so helpful. I'll talk with you soon."

She hurried out of the senior center, letting them return to their card game, while she pondered the idea of a secret room in the tower, and a corresponding one in her inn. Could they be connected and, if so, what could be in them that would make someone like Jim or Nancy Redfield so interested in getting in there? And, even more importantly, could Nancy have been killed over it?

Liz pondered the idea of a room in the clock tower as she went about her afternoon chores. If it was true that Iris went to the tower every day, she must have had a place inside for inclement days. Getting up to the rooms that held the gears and the figurines was a challenge for healthy individuals, with those narrow stairs. The room itself was spacious, if a bit loud when the mechanical gears were working, but there was no way an elderly woman or her elderly father could have made it up there. So that space was out of contention as an option.

That left her with the ground floor. Clearly the Clausens liked secrets, especially if they'd made a secret room in their house. Liz had wandered the tower after the tour and had seen plenty of wall space that might conceal a room. The question should have been easily answered by a look at the architectural drawings of the tower, but Bert had said nothing had been revealed. She decided to ask Melissa Patton once she returned.

She had to wait a while. It was nearly nine o'clock that evening when Melissa closed the front door behind her and headed for the stairs, carrying a stack of papers and a rolled-up document that Liz hoped was the tower plans. Liz cleared her throat carefully, and Melissa jumped, clearly not expecting anyone to be around.

"You startled me, Liz. We had a late meeting with the renovation committee to discuss the plans and the timeline delay due to the...incident."

Liz didn't like hearing Nancy's death termed as just an "incident," but people dealt with death in different ways, she supposed. Right now she needed information. "That's perfect timing. I see you're carrying some documents. Would you happen to have the building plans for the tower?"

Melissa's brow furrowed. "I have them right here. May I ask what you're looking for? Maybe I can help you."

Liz gestured to the table in the dining room beyond. "Well, I did the tour with Bert today, and we were talking about the Clausen family. Apparently, the daughter who commissioned the tower for her father used to go there every day for tea—even after her father had passed. So I was wondering where she might have done that."

Melissa frowned and spread the plans on the table. "I don't have the original plans, unfortunately. I tried to find them in the state records and even in the archives of the papers donated by the Clausen family, but they don't appear to exist. Bert found these plans in his collection. They appear to be copied and are much more recent than the ones that would have been used for the tower. Part of my job is remapping the layout for posterity."

Liz peered at the plans but didn't see any rooms indicated. "Doesn't it seem odd that there aren't any rooms besides the mechanical rooms? I mean, why would they have such a big space and not use it? Wouldn't that have cost more money?"

Melissa eyed her. "It would have been more expensive because they would have needed more building material, that's true." She paused and cast a sideways glance at Liz. "Why the sudden interest in a room there?"

"A few people have asked about the tower and the Clausen family. Rumors hint about valuables and treasure. Surely you've heard about it."

Melissa shrugged. "I don't put much stock in rumors and innuendo. I focus on facts and what I can see."

"So you haven't been poking around for places where there might be space behind walls, and maybe something hidden in that space? I would think finding a treasure trove like that would be very good for your career."

Melissa rolled up the plans and snapped them under her arm. "Are you accusing me of something, Liz? I'm doing my job as a preservationist. I'm supposed to look for places where there are abnormalities and changes in the structure, including weak stonework and other integrity issues. Anything else I find would be incidental to my job at best."

"I meant no offense, truly. If you did happen to find any treasure, who would own that?"

Melissa grew thoughtful. "Well, possession often determines ownership. If it was in a private residence, the owner would have the claim. In a public place like the tower, the town would own it."

"So, you would have no claim to it?" Liz persisted.

Melissa gave her a puzzled look. "Me? Not at all. The most I would get is maybe notoriety as the person who found it. Fodder for a professional article, some publicity—nothing more. But I'm not a treasure hunter. That's not why I'm here." Melissa gave her a pointed look and stalked out of the room.

Liz sighed. She hadn't intended to insult her guest. But at least she'd found out that Melissa's motive was probably not strong enough for murder, even if professional accolades might motivate some people. Melissa didn't seem that type, especially judging by the way she'd stormed off.

On a positive note, Liz had seen the plans, even if they were copies and much later than the original plans. Maybe the state historical society had plans in the architect's papers or in the Clausen collection. She didn't doubt Melissa had checked into that. She wouldn't be a good preservationist if she hadn't. But Liz doubted she would show anyone the real ones if she wanted to find the room herself.

Liz could also try the state university, which had a solid architecture program. They might have a collection of historic building plans, and maybe Melissa hadn't thought to consult them. But that was probably wishful thinking. Melissa seemed very good at her job.

Still, it was worth a try. She would call them tomorrow, speaking as the owner of a house designed and built by the architect and formerly owned by the Clausens. Maybe she'd get lucky.

———————— *⁓⁓⁓⁓⁓⁓⁓⁓* ————————

The next morning, Melissa skipped breakfast and left the inn without a word. Liz knew she should apologize since they'd be stuck together until the renovations were done, or at least until Melissa's part was done. She made a mental note to do so the next time she saw the younger woman.

She retreated to her office to make a few phone calls. The first was to the state historical society.

The woman she spoke to, Doris Tidwell, was apologetic. "We can look through what we have for both the Clausen family and the clock tower, but I doubt we'll find much of anything. It isn't that old, and the Clausens were not a very influential family outside of your town. Iris Clausen did donate some of her father's clocks to our historical society, but they're wasted here. A clock museum would have been a better choice. I can look into our records on the collection and see what we have. The architect, on the other hand, was a bit more famous, and some of his papers and designs might be on record at the university, especially since he designed the main administrative building there."

"Thank you so much," Liz said sincerely. "I would appreciate whatever you can give me. Can you tell me whom I should contact at the university?"

"Sure. I have their information right here. You're not the first person to call about that. Seems like your clock tower is very interesting all of a sudden." Doris laughed.

Liz froze. "We're doing some renovations on it. Could you possibly tell me who might have contacted you about it? I only ask because my house was designed by the same architect, and I wonder if they're asking about my house plans too."

"Sure. Hang on and let me check."

Hold music came on and Liz tapped her fingers on the desk.

After a few minutes, the other woman came back on the line. "I'm sorry. I can't find it at the moment. It must be in the back, and I'm the only one here right now. Can I tell you that when I call back with the research into the collection?"

"Of course," Liz said. "Could you give me the contact at the university?"

She quickly exchanged information with Doris and then hung up. She stared at her notes on the pad. Who would want information on the house or tower plans other than Melissa? Jackson would have mentioned if he had asked about them, or if anyone else had on behalf of the town. Bert would have told her too. Liz had the feeling she was missing something and she wasn't sure what.

She called the university librarian, who confirmed they had a collection that contained many of the architect's plans, but she wasn't sure about the clock tower in Pleasant Creek. The librarian wouldn't win any congeniality awards. According to her, Pleasant Creek's tower was small, insignificant, and designed before the architect became famous. His plans may have been lost—if they'd existed in the first place—or not deemed worthy of inclusion in the collection.

"Is there anyone else who might know anything more about this architect?" Liz was getting frustrated.

"We have a professor who teaches a class on local architects, and he does a segment on your guy, Charles Lawrence. You could contact him, but I can tell you that we have nothing from Pleasant Creek in our collection, so I doubt Dr. McNally has anything new to share."

Liz accepted the professor's phone number and made yet a third call that morning, hoping the professor wasn't as arrogant as the librarian. She left a voice mail explaining who she was and why she was calling, then asked him to call her back.

She felt almost deflated when she hung up. There was nothing more she could do—she'd officially hit a dead end. She decided she deserved a little time with the Material Girls and some quilting therapy.

14

Liz spent the morning with the Mary Ann, working on a quilt and letting her friend's presence comfort her and soothe her disappointment after her fruitless search. After lunch, she headed into town, straight for the tower, stopping at the garden plot to talk with Sadie and see who was hanging around before she went inside. As she admired the gardening work and the way the yellow and orange celosias popped against the purple petunias and green grass, Jim and Kent walked out of the tower. Liz sidled away, ducking a little so she could see them, but they wouldn't see her. Sadie eyed her in confusion but played along, angling her body to help conceal Liz.

Jim and Kent were carrying some tools, and Liz squinted to see what they had. She gestured to them and quietly asked Sadie, "What do you think they're carrying?"

Sadie considered the two men. "It looks like measuring tapes, a camera, and maybe some surveying equipment. I can understand why Kent's there—he's bidding for the contract on the renovation. But why is Jim with him?"

Liz had a good idea. "If I had to guess, I'd say a secret room."

Sadie gaped at her. "That's not a rumor?"

Liz crouched and studied the flowers, pretending not to watch the tower. Sadie followed her lead. "Who knows?" Liz murmured in answer to Sadie's question. "There are plenty of rumors in the world that people still believe. The Holy Grail. UFOs. Why not secret rooms?"

Sadie snorted. "Come on, Liz. A secret room in Pleasant Creek has nothing on any of those other rumors. Those can change the world. Something here is just an oddity."

"Maybe," Liz replied. "But it could change the world for someone. Or at least someone thinks so. Was it enough to kill over?"

"So, you think Nancy was murdered? Stan hasn't actually confirmed it yet, that I know of." Sadie bit her lower lip and looked nervous. She must still wonder how many people thought she'd killed Nancy because of their past feud.

Liz hugged her. "Sadie, no one believes you had anything to do with it. The chief is just doing his duty. If he does it right, your name will be cleared and everyone will know it. Trust Stan."

Sadie tried to smile, but her lips trembled a little. "It's hard, Liz. I know I didn't do anything to cause her death, but I can't really prove it."

"Did you see anyone else in the room or the area, after you argued?"

Sadie stretched her neck. "I've been racking my brain to think of that. I saw a few people when I left the figurines. Jim, that preservationist Melissa, and even that man you have staying at the inn. Kent was wandering around outside too. It's not like the place was buttoned up tight."

It was too much to hope that Sadie had seen someone wearing a sign that said, *I did it*. Well, she was back to square one with the tower. Jim and Kent, after one last glance at the women, separated and moved off, as if satisfied that no one was paying attention to them or was suspicious. Once they were out of sight, Liz stood.

"I'll talk to you later, Sadie. Keep an eye out, okay?"

She headed inside the tower quickly. The stone and brick kept it cool and dark, even with the lights that illuminated the walkway areas. Liz wished had she remembered a flashlight. That would make it easier to study the walls better for any cracks or changes in the stonework. The small windows let in the sunlight, but not enough to see details by.

Liz ran her hands over the stone walls, trying to feel for any changes in the grout or even the stone itself, but she had no luck.

Just beyond the stairs she found a little alcove and felt along the wall. Was that a divot in the stone? She ran her fingers over it again and found an indentation that didn't match the original layer of stone. But the light from the windows didn't quite reach that far. She mentally tagged the spot for a more in-depth visit later, with a powerful flashlight. It would probably turn up nothing. There could be any number of explanations for an anomaly in the stonework—including tourists chipping away at the rock for a souvenir.

Voices alerted her to company. She stepped out from the area to meet Melissa and Jackson, both of whom looked surprised to see her. Liz pasted on a bright smile. "Hi there! Bert got me so interested in the tower's history that I thought I'd stop in quick and take another look around."

Melissa frowned. "You should be careful. There's nothing back there except a dark corner. You could slip and get hurt or something. What were you looking for?"

Liz turned up the wattage on her smile. "Just poking my nose around. But there was nothing there." She shrugged. "I think I'll head to the bakery and see if I can bribe Naomi into parting with a cinnamon roll before I head back home. Have a great day."

"I'll walk you out," Jackson said in a tone that brooked no argument. When they were safely out of the tower, he turned to her and crossed his arms. "Liz, what's going on?"

"I'm just looking around," she repeated.

He wasn't fooled by her innocent explanation. "You're investigating Nancy's death. Why can't you leave it to Stan? Besides, do you really think the tower has anything to do with it?"

"It might if there was a secret room in there and it was linked to the Clausen family. Trust me—Nancy wasn't here at the tower to visit friends, Jackson. She was looking for something. I want to know what it was."

"Maybe it's in the hidden room at the inn," he pointed out.

She wrinkled her nose. "Maybe. We'll open that room up once my lawyer figures out who owns whatever is in there."

Jackson shook his head. "Please be safe. I spoke to the chief. He's definitely treating Nancy's death as a homicide. There almost has to be a connection."

"I know, but don't worry about me. I can hold my own."

Liz studied him, noting the dark circles under his eyes. "Take care of yourself, Jackson. I worry that this special order, not to mention the renovation and other issues, are overextending you."

He managed to give her a smile, albeit a tired one. "It won't be long now. Enjoy your cinnamon roll."

She hugged him, then headed to Sweet Everything. It was quiet at the bakery, so Naomi was able to take a break and visit. She drew Liz into her office to enjoy a cup of coffee and a treat. Naomi toyed with her coffee mug and played with the crumbs on her plate while Liz caught her up. Realizing Naomi wasn't absorbing a word she said, Liz laid a hand on her friend's arm.

"Naomi, is everything okay?"

Naomi sighed heavily and looked into Liz's eyes. It appeared as if the weight of the world was on Naomi's shoulders, judging by the weariness in her eyes. "Liz, is everything okay between you and Jackson? He's been spending more time than usual at Cross Furniture and the town hall. I also know he's been going to the city a lot—I hear plenty of gossip here, as you know. What's going on?"

Liz leaned back in her chair. "We've both been busy, but we're fine. Life happens."

Naomi patted her arm, then took a deep breath, as if the next thing she was going to say took some effort. "He's also been spending time with Sally Van Amburgh in her real estate office. Is he selling his house?"

Now Liz was confused. Jackson had consulted—more than once, apparently—with a realtor? Could he be having more serious financial trouble than he had told her? Perhaps the loan he'd taken out on the special order hadn't been enough—or he needed collateral. But that would be a banking issue, not within Sally's purview. Was business so bad that he had to sell his house to keep afloat? Liz's thoughts spiraled. She wanted to confront Jackson, but clearly there was a reason why he didn't want to tell her. *If it's because he doesn't want me to worry, that's completely failed.*

"I didn't know," Liz confessed. "I don't know why he'd be doing that."

Naomi gripped Liz's hand. "I'm sorry. I didn't know if I should say anything, but if it were me, I'd want to know. Did I do the right thing?"

Liz nodded, a bit preoccupied with her thoughts and worries. "Of course you did, Naomi. But I won't borrow trouble until I'm sure I have something to worry about."

Only, the truth was, Liz had a great deal to worry about on many fronts and she had no idea how to fix any of them.

After she left Naomi's bakery, needing exercise to clear her head, she decided to head to her lawyer's office for an update. As she passed the small driveway between buildings, she did a double take. Tom, her lawyer, was talking with Jim and Kent. She lingered along the edge of the building, trying to eavesdrop on the conversation, but they were speaking too quietly.

She leaned against the building and tried to cope with what she'd seen. She had known that Jim had friends in town, and Kent knew everyone. There were only a couple of lawyers in town, and it was reasonable that Kent or Jim could have business with Tom separate from her own. She would expect her lawyer to work in her best interests, not someone else's, which he was ethically bound to do, and to recuse himself if a conflict of interest arose.

But now she had to wonder about that nonstandard clause in the real estate agreement. Surely Tom would have known if something like that had been requested by the seller and should have told her. So how had it gotten there? A disturbing possibility occurred to her, one that would require a call to the office of the Indiana State Bar Association.

Could the clause have been placed there at Jim and Nancy Redfield's request?

Or had it been Kent's idea?

———————————— //////////////////////////// ————————————

Liz went back to the inn, still stewing about what she'd seen. Short of demanding her lawyer tell her what business he had with Kent or Jim or both—which would be pointless, as he'd certainly claim attorney-client privilege—there was nothing she could do about it without proof. Just talking to people on the street didn't mean her lawyer wasn't doing her job.

Needing to do something proactive, she decided to go back to the tower, this time with a flashlight. It was unlikely she'd find anything when the professionals hadn't—or if the professionals had found something, they weren't talking—but it was worth a try.

When she arrived, she slipped through the door and stopped short. It seemed someone else had had the same idea.

Pete McConnell was absorbed in inspecting the wall under the stairs with a small penlight, checking out the grooves in particular. Periodically he pulled out a small, old notebook and squinted at the writing, then back at the wall. Voices from people passing outside suddenly echoed around the small space and his head jerked up. He froze like a deer in headlights when he saw her.

Liz advanced slowly. "Do you need more light?"

He watched her for a long moment, then nodded.

She pulled out her flashlight and trained it on the spot he had been examining, and he bent closer to peer carefully at the mortar work. Finally, he stood to his full height.

"Did you find what you were looking for?"

He shrugged. "I'm not sure. This spot has potential. But it seems an awkward place and too small. It could be from a prior renovation and repair work."

"How did you know where to look?" Liz asked, wondering if he'd share any information when he'd been so secretive before.

"My grandfather was from around here. He told me stories of growing up here."

"You've told me that. Who was he, Pete? The truth this time." She tried to infuse her tone with authority, willing him to tell her everything.

He cast her a sideways glance. "My grandfather worked for the Clausens. Nancy recognized the name."

"Michael McConnell."

Pete nodded. "Yes. He told me about coming here every day with Miss Iris."

"Did he say what was in the room?"

Pete grimaced and shook his head. "No, only that they had tea every day. But I know that Ralph Clausen collected clocks and watches, many of them valuable."

"Why didn't you tell me this before?"

Pete shrugged. "I didn't want to talk about it, I guess. I wanted to find out if the stories were even true. But then Nancy Redfield recognized my name."

"What did it matter if she recognized your name?"

"She owed my grandfather, my family. She stole the money Iris wanted my grandfather to have as a pension and the items he was supposed to have. He always said he didn't care about the money, but he should have spent the rest of his days in comfort. I only wanted what was due to my family. I want him to have the kind of final resting place he deserved." The words rushed out of Pete in a flood.

She stared at the anguish on his face and felt a rush of sympathy for him. "I'm so sorry, Pete. I had no idea. Was it written in her will?"

He gave a bitter laugh. "As if that would matter. Nancy had all the money, controlled the lawyers, had access to the house and the finances. My grandfather had nothing. He fulfilled Iris's wish to seal a certain room intact, and then he left. But Iris must have left him something. Somewhere."

"Have you been searching my house for clues too?"

A guilty flush spread up his neck and he nodded sheepishly. "I'm sorry. Grandfather struggled so much after he left here. He devoted so many years to that family, only to be turned away as if he were a beggar."

"Did you see Nancy Redfield the day of her death?"

Pete's eyes widened, and a hint of fear entered them. "I don't know what you're talking about."

"You were seen in the tower that day, right before her death. Did you speak with her?"

"I don't recall." His voice was shaky but he met her gaze firmly. "I have to go."

His words rang false to Liz, but she decided not to call him on it at that moment. She stepped aside to allow him to pass her. He paused at the door and looked back at her over his shoulder.

"I only wanted what was owed my grandfather." Then he left the tower.

When Liz made it back to the inn later that afternoon, she found chaos waiting for her. Jim was in the rotunda, pacing back and forth, his face red with anger. Beans was glaring at his former owner from his favorite rug in the corner of the foyer, emitting low growls from time to time.

"Well, it's about time," Jim snapped at her. "While you've been gallivanting about, someone broke into that third-floor room and through that wall."

Just the way she liked to be greeted in her own home. She set her bag on the front desk and dug deep to find her patience.

When she was confident in her ability to speak reasonably, she said, "Jim, as you know, we were aware that someone had tried to get through the wall, but we put a new lock on the door. I can assure you, I have not allowed anyone in there."

"Well, someone has been in there." He tossed the metal padlock on the front desk and it landed with a loud thud, making a gouge in the soft wood.

Liz stared at the padlock as if it were a viper. "What do you mean? You found the door unlocked?"

He huffed. "Yes, I went upstairs to check on the room and the lock was broken, hanging like this. When I went inside, there was a hole drilled all the way through, but not big enough to see anything, even if there had been light. My lawyer is going to hear about this."

Anger burned in her stomach. "Which lawyer is that, Jim?" He didn't flinch so she couldn't tell if she'd hit her mark. She continued.

"So, you went into the room when no one is supposed to be in there? How do I know that you didn't break into the room yourself?"

He pulled himself up, seeming a couple of inches taller. "How dare you! I would never do that."

Liz stalked up the stairs, Jim hot on her heels. Sure enough, the door was open, which she expected since Jim had given her the padlock. Inside, the hole that she and Jackson had found was bigger and now went all the way through, but it still wasn't big enough to see anything. Perhaps if she had a tiny camera or a telescoping lens.

She turned and almost bumped into Jim, who stood far too close.

"You have not kept up your end of the bargain," he growled. "My lawyer will have something to say about this."

"Your lawyer will have nothing to say about this because you can't prove to me that you didn't do it, and right now, I've had it. Tomorrow morning, that wall is coming down." She no longer cared who owned what, if anything, was on the other side. She'd deal with it when the time came.

A triumphant gleam entered Jim's face and he smiled. "Great. I'll call Kent."

"No, I will make arrangements to have this done, and we will all be present. Please respect my decision, Jim." Liz tried for a professional tone, but she was weary of this whole business. "Coffee hour starts soon downstairs. After that, I'll see you in the morning."

Jim apparently sensed that he was near his goal because he withdrew without another word. Liz headed downstairs to call Jackson and Steve and enlist their aid in tearing down the wall tomorrow. Jackson agreed immediately and said he was coming over to check out the wall again to see what tools he might need for the demolition.

He arrived within the hour with yet another lock and some tools to set up. Steve arrived a short time later. Liz put together something for dinner for the three of them in the kitchen, while Steve and Jackson laid out a tarp in the closet and prepared for the demolition of the wall.

Finally, they came downstairs and dug into the hearty roast beef sandwiches and the peach pie Mary Ann had left on the kitchen counter earlier that day. Steve took his sandwich and pie to go, saying, with a wink at his boss, that he had to get to work. After Liz and Jackson finished, they lingered over his coffee in the library, enjoying the silence and the company.

Liz debated over saying anything, noting how tired Jackson looked. She remembered Naomi's words from earlier in the day, and Jackson's distance over his own issues. Finally, she couldn't stop the words. "I know you've been talking to Sally Van Amburgh. I can't imagine it's about town business. What's going on?"

He scrubbed a hand over his face and avoided looking at her. "It's nothing. I'm just exploring some options."

Liz leaned across the small table between their chairs and laid a hand on his arm, feeling his muscles bunch under her fingers. "Don't cut me out of this, Jackson. I want to help you."

He laid a hand on top of hers and gripped it tightly. "I care about you, Liz. You know that, right? Can you trust me when I say that this is nothing you can help me with, that I will tell you what I can when I can?"

She pulled away, sighing. "Jackson, I'm worried about you. You're working so hard and seem so tired. You're taking out loans, going into the city all the time, and now looking at selling your home. I can't help but wonder if everything is okay."

He smiled at her, stood, and pulled her to her feet. He wrapped his arms around her and drew her close. She rested her head against his shoulder. "Just knowing you're here and supporting me is exactly what I need," he said quietly. "I promise you, when I can share more, I will. Will you trust me?"

She lifted her head and peered into his face. "I'll always trust you, Jackson. Just don't push me away."

"Never."

———————— *//////////////////////////* ————————

That night, after Jackson left, Liz did her customary last walk around the inn before bed. Beans trotted behind, almost as if he were guarding her, then waited at the bottom of the staircase when she went to check the upstairs.

She'd almost finished walking through the second floor when something clattered to the floor overhead. A chill ran up her spine, and she wondered if maybe she shouldn't be doing this walk-through. But that thought was quickly followed by the reality that if she didn't do it, who else would?

Besides, maybe it was her overactive imagination playing tricks on her. Pete McConnell was staying up there and he'd probably dropped something again, as he had in the library. Only it sounded as if it had come from across the hall, and no one had business being there. She headed up the stairs, determined to catch someone in the act. But when she got up there, the door was locked. There were marks on the door, but Liz couldn't be sure if they were from the prior damage, the installation of the new lock, or from another attempt at breaking in.

She knocked on Pete's door. After a long moment, he opened it, blinking blearily at her as if he'd just woken up.

"I'm so sorry to bother you. Did you hear anything up here a few minutes ago? Or did something fall in your room?"

He yawned. "I was asleep until you knocked. I didn't hear a thing."

She glanced down at the hand that rested on his doorknob. Scratches marred his forearm, something she hadn't noticed earlier in the day because he'd been wearing a jacket. "What happened to your arm? Do you need some first-aid cream?"

He glanced down and yanked his arm back. "I was petting a cat in town and it scratched me. It will be fine."

The scratches weren't uniform or parallel and hadn't looked like they came from an animal's claw. But she let it go. "Cat scratches can get infected quickly. Let me know if you need any ointment or disinfectant."

He nodded and closed the door. A creak on the stairs made Liz turn and dart back down to the second floor in time to see the door of the Rose of Sharon Room click shut. Liz narrowed her eyes. Melissa's room. Had Melissa been upstairs or was she just getting back from wherever she had been? She hadn't been there earlier in the evening so it was possible that she came from downstairs and not the third floor. Liz was tempted to knock, but decided against it. Tomorrow, they'd open the wall and it would be over.

She hoped.

———— //////////////////////// ————

After breakfast the next morning, all interested parties gathered on the third floor: Jim, Kent, both sides' lawyers, along with Jackson and Steve. Kent had a sour look on his face and glowered at everyone as if he was angry that someone else was getting to do the work. Liz still wasn't convinced he hadn't given the tools to Jim or helped Jim drill through the wall to see what was on the other side.

But that was all in the past now. They were getting inside the space, no matter the legalities, the ownership issues, or anything else. And maybe they'd find the answers they were all looking for. Liz couldn't decide if she wanted the room to be empty, or to contain something wonderful. Empty would be easiest, at least for her.

Melissa Patton also lingered on the fringes of the crowd, standing on tiptoe to get a better look. Bert Worth had been invited because he would appreciate the historic moment. As a result, the third-floor hallway was quite crowded and some people weren't going to get to see much at all.

"If I had been asked, I could have had this wall torn down in no time," Kent declared loudly to anyone who would listen.

Liz shot him a look. "I think you can see that we could never work together. It's better this way."

He glared. "You may change your mind yet." He stepped closer so only Liz could hear him. "You might need the money from the sale of this place someday. Don't alienate the one person willing to buy it from you."

"We've been through this, Kent. I won't ever sell the inn to you so you can tear it down."

"Then you'll be surrounded by a housing development. How much business do you think you'd get then? What will your guests think of the view of a series of houses around you?"

He had to be bluffing. There was no way he had enough land—any land—to make the development a reality. Or did he? Had one of her neighbors caved to his pressure? Maybe she needed to talk with the Bielers again and make sure they hadn't given in.

The wall demolition took a bit longer than expected. Jackson started by pulling away some of the old wallpaper, revealing an old door that had been painted over. He broke through the paint seal, which had already cracked a bit and, through a bit of good old-fashioned force, they were able to open the door. Jim attempted to push his way in and be the first through, but Liz and Jackson stepped between him and the door.

"My house, my room," Liz said firmly.

The lawyers stared at her. When she stared back, her lawyer

glanced away, flushing under her scrutiny. It confirmed her suspicions that he had been influenced by the Redfields in some way to put in that clause in the sale documents and not point it out to her. He was looking at a grievance with the state bar commission and he knew it. It all depended on the next several minutes.

Jackson used a crowbar to pry open the door, since the doorknob was long gone, probably removed when the room had been sealed. With a crack, the rest of the paint seal around the door gave way and the door stood ajar. Jackson and Steve worked together to open it more fully, but only left enough space for Liz to go inside. When she had slipped through, they acted as a barrier so no one else could join her.

Liz turned on the flashlight she carried and scanned the room. A heavy layer of dust coated the surface, but it was clear what the room was supposed to be. A dresser stood against one wall, ornately carved and clearly an antique. Next to it was a beautiful rocking chair made of a dark wood, possibly walnut.

But what Liz saw against the far wall made her stomach clench.

A blanket was still draped over the crib, although the blanket was ratty now. When Liz stepped into the room more fully, she could see more items for a baby. A rocking horse, hand-painted with real hair for the mane and tail. A doll on another chair. A small table-and-chair set. A tiny bookcase.

Liz pressed a hand to her stomach and resisted the urge to cry. Her eyes burned with unshed tears as she took in the scene. Jackson appeared beside her and laid an arm across her shoulder, offering silent comfort.

Jim pushed his way in and stared. "I wonder if this was Iris's room when she was a baby."

"She never lived here as a baby. This house was built when she was older. No baby ever lived in this house," Bert said quietly from Liz's other side.

"Well, someone expected to have a baby here," Liz stated.

All eyes turned to Jim, who was staring wide-eyed at the room. "It wasn't us. I never even knew this room existed."

Melissa stepped forward. "This furniture is too old for Jim and Nancy to have used it. Could it have been Iris who was having a baby?"

Jim shrugged. "I don't think she ever had children. She never married."

"You don't need to be married to have children," Melissa retorted.

"In those days you did. Besides, Nancy was her cousin. Wouldn't she have known about a baby? Wouldn't the baby have inherited this place?"

"If the baby had lived," Pete said.

Everyone jumped. Liz hadn't known Pete was even there. He hadn't been in the hallway with everyone else. In fact, Liz had wondered if he had left before they had started their work.

Pete held up the notebook that Liz recognized as the one he'd been referring to when he was inspecting the tower. "This notebook belonged to my grandfather. He was Michael McConnell. Remember him, Mr. Redfield? The man you and your wife tricked out of his rightful inheritance from Iris?"

Jim had the grace to flush and look away. But Pete wasn't done yet. "My grandfather loved Iris Clausen and was dedicated to the family. He told me that Iris had once been in love and had gotten pregnant while her father was traveling for business in Europe before the war. I don't know if her father ever knew about the pregnancy because she made arrangements to go off and live with a sympathetic relative on the East Coast for the last few weeks of her pregnancy. But the baby died there, and when she returned, she had my grandfather seal the room."

"Who was the father?" Liz asked, though she had a guess.

Pete smiled, as if reading her mind. "My grandfather never said. I often wondered if it was him, but he only said the father of the child died in the war. So many young men died during the war that it was possible. I only know that her father would have never approved of the marriage."

Everyone looked around the room. The almost palpable excitement from earlier had been replaced with sadness for the poor woman who had lost both her child and the love of her life. By unspoken agreement, everyone filed out of the room, closing the door behind them. Liz wasn't sure what she'd do with the room or its contents now that she knew what was in there, but that was a decision for another day.

As she passed Pete on her way out, Liz glanced at him, and what she saw on his face made her pause.

He looked haunted.

16

After everyone left, Liz felt oddly deflated. She sat in her office for a long time doing nothing, then decided she needed company. She headed to the shop, but even quilting didn't quite help soothe her spirit this time. So, she sat and let the conversations wash over her, soaking up the comfort of her friends' presence.

She'd been there for about an hour when her cousin Miriam came in. Apparently sensing Liz was troubled, she patted her arm. Liz quickly outlined what they had found upstairs, and Miriam's eyes filled with tears. Losing a child was something everyone could relate to, and even though Miriam hadn't known Iris, she sympathized with the woman.

She clutched Liz's hand and bit her lower lip. "I really hate to ask this, Liz. But Susannah Bieler came to see me yesterday. She seems to think you changed your mind and you're selling the inn. Are you?"

Liz was surprised. "Of course not. I told Susannah I wasn't selling. Are they?"

Miriam looked troubled. "She says they're considering it. If you're going to be gone, they don't want to be surrounded by a housing development."

Kent's words came back to Liz from that morning. That man was playing them off each other, keeping her occupied elsewhere while he convinced the Bielers that she was selling! Anger burned in her chest. She stood.

"Miriam, I think I need to go speak with Susannah and her husband. I have no intention of selling, especially now and especially not to Kent McInerney. Thank you for letting me know. I'll head over there right now."

Miriam hugged her again. "Thank you so much. Susannah is so worried. That farm is all they have. They're hoping one of the young men from another family will come and take over eventually, help them with it when they're older, then buy them out. They don't want to sell it to Kent for development."

Still angry, Liz headed straight to the Bielers' farm. When she pulled into their drive, Kent's truck was there and he was just getting out. His gaze narrowed when he spied her. "What are you doing here?"

"Making sure you don't keep playing your games between us. Are you telling the Bielers that I am selling to you?"

He shrugged. "Everyone knows your boyfriend has been taking out a loan for his business and looking at selling his house. It's a safe bet that business is tough and he could use an influx of cash. I know you care about him. It's possible you'd sell the inn to help him out."

"That's an awful lot of assumptions, Kent. Are you telling me you never take out business loans for any of your projects? You never took out a loan to buy property, hoping to pay it off when you sold the development? Stop playing games or I might have to contact the state licensing board and report you for unethical business practices."

He glared at her. "You have nothing on me. This is how business works."

"Not here, Kent. Get back in your truck and leave."

He opened the truck door and swung in. "This isn't over, Liz."

"For you it is. Don't come back. I'm not selling to you, and neither are the Bielers. Your development is sunk before it's even begun."

He tore out of the driveway, dust billowing behind him. When he was gone, Liz saw Susannah and her husband, Abram, standing on their porch, hope in their eyes.

"You truly aren't selling?"

She walked over to them. "Of course not. I have no intentions of it, especially not to him."

"But the things he said about Jackson Cross and his business. If you marry him, won't you sell your business and move in with him?"

She smiled. "No. He knows how much I love the inn. I can keep my own business and he'll have his. We'll work it out. Jackson's business is doing just fine, no matter what Kent says. Don't listen to him. I'm so sorry I haven't had a chance to touch base with you since last time. If I had known what he was doing, I could have alleviated your worries long before now."

"That's fine. We appreciate you coming here now. Thank you so much. Would you stay for some pie?"

"I'd love some." Liz sat in the kitchen and enjoyed a pleasant morning visiting with her neighbors, a couple she hadn't spent much time with prior to this week. She vowed to ensure they remained close friends from now on.

As she was getting ready to leave, she decided to take a stab in the dark. "Did you or your family know the Clausens well, particularly Iris?"

Abram froze. "Why do you ask?"

"Just this morning, we opened up a hidden room in the inn that had been sealed for years. It was intended to be a nursery, only no one ever seems to know anything about a baby in the house. We wondered what the story was there."

Abram and Susannah exchanged glances. Susannah gave a small nod and Abram sighed. "My father spoke about his brother, who left the community and was close to Iris Clausen. He rejected our ways, and my father said he intended to marry an English woman. My father thought it was Iris. But he was drafted to the war. Since he wasn't in the community, he couldn't claim religious exemption and had to go."

"You think the baby was his?"

Abram nodded soberly. "It's possible, but we'll never know for sure."

"That's so sad," Liz commented. "Thank you for letting me know."

"We would appreciate it if you didn't say anything about this to others. My father didn't want the story shared."

"I understand." Liz paused. "Iris wanted the baby. She must have loved it very much, judging by the room she prepared."

Abram smiled. "I'm glad. I didn't know my uncle, but my father grieved him for the rest of his life—both his leaving the community and his death in the war."

Liz drove away, thinking about how sad the whole story was. Yet she still didn't have an answer as to what everyone was looking for. It was clear that a nursery was not what Jim had expected to be on the other side of the wall. So, what was he looking for? The furniture could be worth some money, as antiques, but not enough to be the valuables rumored to be hidden somewhere in the house or tower. If there was some sort of treasure, it had to be in the tower then.

Liz suspected the mystery wasn't over. It had only moved and refocused from her inn to the clock tower.

Back at the inn, Liz sat in her kitchen enjoying a cup of tea, along with Sadie and Mary Ann. Sadie had finally returned to the quilt shop and the inn to report that the garden plot was just about done. They chatted idly about the room and how no one knew Iris had once been pregnant.

"That's not surprising really," Mary Ann said. "Back then, she could have worn clothes to hide it, and no one would notice because she was a recluse. They might think she'd gained weight but that's it."

"What about the father?" Sadie asked.

Liz couldn't divulge what the Bielers suspected, so she simply told a version of the truth. "I guess we'll never know for sure who that was. But he apparently wasn't in the picture."

"She never married, so he either died or left. She was left alone to mourn all those years. Poor Iris. No wonder she was eccentric toward the end," Mary Ann said.

"Well, none of these answers the mystery of why Nancy died," Liz replied, frustrated.

"Do we even know it was murder and not an accident? Have you talked to Stan recently?"

Liz paused, thinking about the last time she had talked to him. "You know, I haven't spoken to him recently. Jackson said they're treating it as a homicide, but that could just be erring on the side of caution. We're assuming she was murdered, but she could have tripped, I suppose."

"If she was murdered, and I know I didn't do it, why would someone hurt her, besides her nasty personality? I mean, she didn't really see anyone once she was back in town, except us," Sadie said.

"Well, she saw Jim and Kent and her lawyer. She could have seen other people. I haven't even checked into her movements." Liz felt like smacking herself in the head. How could she have missed that? Some sleuth she was.

"Have you tried looking in the boxes? Maybe there's a clue in there," Mary Ann suggested. "I know you're trying to be nice and there was that legal clause, but honestly, has anyone examined the contents?"

Liz thought about it. Jim hadn't even asked about the boxes with how focused he'd been on the room, and that's what the legal documents were about. Clearly they weren't important to him. The boxes had only been the vehicle to try to get control of the room.

"That's a great point. I need to go through them, but technically, I'm still bound by the legal clause in the sale documents until Jim releases me. But I have a plan."

A smile spread across her face as the idea formed in her mind.

Mary Ann and Sadie exchanged glances, Sadie with a gleam of excitement and Mary Ann with resignation.

Liz headed up to Jim's room and knocked on his door.

He opened the door and scowled at her. "Happy about the room? There's nothing in there."

"Actually, I think it's very sad. I feel so bad for Iris, to have that heartache and no one to share it with. Not even family."

He winced as the barb hit home. "She wasn't one to let anyone close. What can I do for you?" He stood back and ushered her into the room.

"The chief has released Nancy's room, so I need to get in there and clean it. Do you know who her heir is?"

"I already told you it's me. Neither of us ever changed our wills. I checked into that when I made her funeral arrangements. Her lawyer contacted me with the details. I have no use for women's clothes. You can donate them. I would like her jewelry, I suppose."

"I'd prefer to go through the room with you, to ensure that there are no questions over where anything went. I know this is a difficult time, but this needs to be done."

"Fine. Let's do it."

He walked over to his desk to pick up something and Liz saw a picture that caught her attention. "It looks like a newspaper article." She scanned the caption. "It's about Iris." The photo was clearly taken in her later years. She was tiny, wrapped in a shawl. Her face was sad but beautiful at the same time.

He barely glanced at it. "I suppose. It's nothing. Just a piece of paper. With no value whatsoever. Kent said Nancy gave it to him, then he gave it back to me. I have no idea why."

She peered at it closer. "I'd love to have it for the inn, as part of the history. Would you consider letting me make a copy?"

"Sure." He handed it to her and headed out of the room, toward the Heirloom Room. "I can start sorting her things while you copy it."

She nodded and opened the door to Nancy's room for him. He paused in the doorway, as if visibly shaken. He took a deep breath and then walked inside, his hands trembling slightly. The door closed behind him and Liz headed downstairs to make a copy of the article. Interesting that Kent had claimed Nancy gave it to him. Liz was under the impression that Nancy couldn't stand Kent and the feeling was entirely mutual.

What if she didn't give it to him willingly?

———— *//////////////////////////* ————

Liz was standing by the copier when Sadie walked in. "What do you have there?"

Liz handed her the article. "Jim had this picture of Iris in his room. It must have been important, but I can't figure out why."

Sadie examined the paper. "I remember this. Iris gave an interview about the clocks her father collected. I often wondered where they all went."

"She donated them to the state historical society," Liz said. "I called them."

An idea had started forming in Liz's mind, the rumor about the treasure poking at her. What if Iris hadn't donated *all* the clocks? Some Swiss watches, she knew, were extremely valuable.

"Hey Liz, look at this," Sadie said, pointing to the article.

For the first time, Liz noticed that the article gave a list of the clocks owned by Ralph Clausen. A few of the entries had a little asterisk next to them, clearly made with a pen. "Sadie, do you think it's possible that some of these clocks could still be in Pleasant Creek, possibly hidden somewhere? Maybe that's what Nancy was looking for. Maybe she was looking for the clocks that are marked on this article."

Sadie cocked her head, a thoughtful look on her face. "You know, that might make sense. But I'm still not sure if you'd know what was missing, even with this list."

Liz looked at the picture. "I wonder if some of these clocks in the photograph are the missing ones. According to this article, these are very rare, from Europe. The state historical society said they didn't display them, that they belonged in a clock museum. Who knows if they're even inventoried, or just sitting around in boxes somewhere there?"

"Good point. So you think the clocks might be the hidden treasure that everyone keeps talking about?

"Could be," said Liz. "Guess we'll have to find out, won't we?"

Liz made a copy of the article and also scanned it to her computer, intending to send it to Doris at the state historical society to see if she recognized the clocks in their collection. Before she went back upstairs, she ran through the downstairs to check if any of the clocks were from the picture. None of them were, but Liz knew she was onto something. It felt like this was the missing piece.

When she went back upstairs, Jim was still in the Heirloom Room. She knocked, and he called for her to enter. He was sitting on the bed with a small pile of valuables on the comforter next to him, mostly jewelry and money. The boxes were still in her quarters downstairs. Liz wondered now if some of the clocks—smaller ones—or watches could be hidden in them.

She handed him the article and he carefully placed it with the items. "I don't know what to do with the rest of her things," he confessed. "I have no need for her clothes or anything. I've gone through what she has."

"Does she have friends back home who might want these?"

He gave her a sad smile. "Doubtful. Nancy had acquaintances, but went through people faster than most people go through socks. No one stayed long because she could be a bit difficult, as I'm sure you saw. She made no provisions for anyone else in her will."

Liz nodded slowly, Naomi's charity that provided housing and furniture to homeless families coming to mind. "We could donate her things to a local charity. One of my friends runs it. Nancy had some beautiful clothes. I'm sure they'd be appreciated."

He looked up at her. "Would you do that? I would be so grateful for your help."

"Of course. We could send her things to the group, if you're sure." She paused, thinking about the boxes that had been found on the third floor and were still in her quarters. "What about the boxes?"

He shook his head. "It's just papers, right? They were her family things, not mine. You can have them. Besides, they started this whole mess. Somehow I feel as if they're cursed. I'll withdraw all legal claim to them. I'll make sure my lawyer handles it immediately."

"Thank you. I will take care of all of it today."

He stood. "Me too. I will talk to my lawyer. I doubt I'll be here more than another couple of days. We're having a small service the day after tomorrow and burying her here. I don't know where else to do it."

The sadness in him tugged at Liz's heart, despite everything he had put her through. "Is there anything else I can do for you?"

He smiled ruefully. "No, you've been wonderful, despite the situation. Thank you."

He left the room, clutching the small pile of valuables and the article. Liz carefully locked the door behind her. She had other things to take care of first before she dug into the boxes.

Later that day, Liz called Bert and asked to meet him at the courthouse, where he housed most of the town's papers. He seemed surprised by her request, but met her at the archives an hour later. She showed him the article and asked specifically about the clocks in the picture. He pulled out a magnifying glass and peered closer, then shook his head.

"I don't recall seeing any of these clocks in anything she donated to the town. We do have two of her father's clocks here, but they're not particularly valuable—no more so than any other antique clock anyway. As far as I know everything went to the state historical society." He sat back in his chair, the coils squeaking.

"But what if they didn't all go there? Do you know what could have happened to them?"

"Well, this was an article specifically on the clocks themselves and the collectible nature of them. It's always possible she was approached after it was published to sell them or donate them to a clock museum. Iris would have donated them rather than sell them, but I would think there would be a record of that."

Liz frowned. "I plan to look in some boxes that were left behind to see if there were any documents about that or anything else. But you have a record of some of what she donated. Are there any mentions of places other than here and the state historical society?"

Bert pulled out a document. "I checked my records after we talked last, and I have no other places listed. I also checked for any clock museums around at the time she was alive and there's nothing in the area. If she did donate, the place would be obscure, far away, or no longer around. Sorry, Liz."

Her shoulders slumped. "That's okay, Bert. I appreciate you trying. Back to square one."

"Do you really think the clocks are important?"

She shrugged and carefully put the article away. "I don't know. But I can't think of anything else connected to the Clausens that would be valuable enough for someone to hurt someone else over, if that's even what happened. Can you?"

Bert shook his head. "No, I can't. But who would do that? I mean, Nancy and Jim would have inherited the clocks. They're probably long gone by now, sold off years ago if Nancy ever had them."

Liz couldn't shake the feeling that the marked clocks in the article were tied to what was going on in her inn and Nancy's death, although she didn't know for sure if it was murder. She thanked Bert, left the courthouse, and then headed directly to the police station, where she cornered Stan in his office.

"I wondered when you'd come to see me. It's not like you to sit idly by when one of your guests has died, even if I wish you'd leave the sleuthing to the police," Stan said, a smile on his face.

Liz sat down. "I would have dropped in sooner, but I've been busy with a few things at the inn. Jim mentioned that he was ready for the memorial service, so I figured you had the report on Nancy's death. Was she murdered?"

Stan sighed and he opened a folder. "That's a really good question, Liz. Basically, the medical examiner said the death was blunt-force trauma, but he couldn't say if she was hit or pushed or fell on her own. So, we're treating it as a suspicious death and investigating it as such. But she had no defensive wounds or any other indication of foul play."

"Beyond her death." Liz pointed out.

"Beyond her death," Stan agreed. "So, we're not really sure which direction to go, to be honest. It could have been an accident. We'll keep looking into it, but we might never find out what really happened."

"Is Sadie still a suspect? I know this is really bothering her, Stan."

Stan's expression softened. "I know, Liz. I can't imagine her doing it, but Kent was pretty insistent he heard them arguing and thought he heard Nancy cry out."

"Then why didn't he go in there and check on her?"

Stan shrugged. "I asked him the same question. He said he and Nancy never really got along. She'd never appreciate his poking his nose in."

Liz shook her head. "If only he had gone in there. Maybe she lost her balance, and he could have helped her."

"We may never know," Stan replied sadly.

"I know you're not supposed to say anything, but did Nancy have anything on her, like pictures or notes or something?"

"Nothing out of the ordinary. Why?"

Liz sighed. Another dead end. "No reason. I'm just trying to figure out what Nancy was doing in the tower."

Stan chuckled. "That's an excellent question. If you find an answer, please let me know."

"I will. Is Jim Redfield free to go?"

"Yup, he can leave, and all of Nancy's things have been released to him as of yesterday. I gave him everything she had on her person when she died."

"Thanks, Stan. I'll let you know if I think of anything."

Liz left the police station more frustrated than ever. She felt like she was so close, but a critical piece of the puzzle was missing and she had no idea what it could be. Perhaps this was one mystery destined to go unsolved.

Liz walked down the street, thinking of getting some lunch at Mama's Home Cooking, when she ran into Pete McConnell. He was standing outside the place, as if debating whether to go inside. Liz had been watching him and noticed he didn't really talk to too many people, as if he was too shy or nervous to speak to others. But an image flashed in her mind from earlier in the day—the look on his face when he had seen the hidden nursery.

That same haunted look was on his face now, and she made a split-second decision.

"Pete, why don't you join me for lunch? We had a rough morning, and I could use some comfort food. Mama's makes the best."

Pete seemed about to make an excuse, then sighed. "Sounds good, Liz. Thank you."

They found a booth toward the back and each ordered a sandwich. Liz chatted about the town and asked him about what he had been doing since he'd been there, but Pete wasn't too open about his plans. Finally, after their drinks had been delivered, Liz decided to ask the question that had been bugging her.

"You seemed a bit shaken up this morning. Seeing that nursery was so sad, wasn't it?"

His eyes took on a faraway look and he nodded. "It didn't seem real until I saw it for myself. She must have loved the baby very much."

"I'm sure she did. Look at the care she put into that room. So sad to lose the child after all of that." Liz studied Pete closely and was rewarded when he flinched as if struck physically. "You said your grandfather told you about the baby? He knew Iris well and was around when she was pregnant?"

Pete nodded. "He really cared about her, I think. He took care of her until she passed."

"He gave up a lot for her. A family. A life. He must have loved her very much." Liz waited until Pete's head came up and his gaze met hers bleakly.

"You didn't tell us everything this morning, did you?" Liz reached across the table and gripped his hand. "Are you related to Iris Clausen?"

He nodded. "My father was her baby."

Liz put the pieces together in an instant. "Hers and your grandfather's. The baby never died. She gave him up for adoption because she knew she could never marry your grandfather and couldn't raise a child on her own."

Pete nodded sadly in agreement. "It wasn't done back then. Besides, my grandfather said he was beneath her socially. Her father would have disowned her. When he came back from Europe, he was so sick. She needed to stay and take care of him. They gave the baby to a young family with the agreement to leave and never come back."

"Abram Bieler's brother?"

Pete nodded again. "He took the baby and left the community with a local woman he had wanted to marry, outside the Amish. But then he was killed in the war. My grandfather helped support my father and his adopted mother until my father was old enough to be on his own, but he stayed in touch. After he left Pleasant Creek, my grandfather came to live with us. He told me about my grandmother, and I wanted to come here and see the town for myself."

"Did you talk to Nancy or Jim about who you were?"

He looked horrified. "Of course not. I don't want anything. I just want to know who she was."

The waitress took that moment to bring the food. As they ate, Liz couldn't help but wonder if Pete was telling the whole truth. Just a few days prior, he had stated that the Redfields had cheated his grandfather out of money and an inheritance from Iris. Now he claimed to want nothing? It seemed too easy. She'd have to look into his story some more, especially if he could have a better claim on the Clausen estate if anything new was found. Jim's claim as ex-husband and heir to Nancy's estate would fall by the wayside if Pete could prove his story.

Could the Redfields have suspected?

Liz headed back to the inn, and Sarah met her at the desk with a message from the state historical society. She went into her office and called them back, hoping for good news. She sat at her desk and childishly crossed her fingers as she dialed.

Doris Tidwell answered on the second ring and greeted her warmly. "Well, your little town has certainly had quite a bit of interest in the past couple of weeks. Lots of people have been inquiring on the clock tower and your inn. I can tell you with little doubt that we do not have your house plans on file, nor does the library."

"What about the clock tower?"

"That's a bit more interesting. I hear your town is doing renovations on it. Well, some of the requests have been in relation to that project, including from a Kent McInerney and a Melissa Patton. They were both clear on what they needed it for, but we all know Melissa here anyway, so she was never a problem."

"What do you mean you know Melissa?"

"She was an intern here while she was a student at the university, and she did her thesis on your architect, Charles Lawrence. She tried to prove he was revolutionary—before his time as an architect. Personally, I didn't think her thesis held water, but Dr. McNally was her advisor and she probably did it to get a better grade. Although, one of my colleagues said Melissa was descended from that architect and wanted to prove something about him. Who knows?"

Charles Lawrence, the architect, was Melissa's ancestor? What else hadn't she told Liz? "What did she want to prove? Do you recall?" Liz insisted.

"Well, I don't remember exactly. Just that the clock tower wasn't some throwaway work, a stone block in some tiny town. She said he built it as a smaller version of some clock tower in Europe, and it had some interesting elements that made it more than just a basic building. And her thesis talked about a legend of secret rooms and hiding places. All conspiracy theories, if you ask me. Nothing came of it. If she had had anyone else for an advisor, she probably would have failed." Doris paused. "The other man was a bit different."

"Kent?" Liz asked.

"Yes. He didn't want to leave his driver's license or tell us who he was or why he wanted the plans, not that he had to tell us why. He just had to prove who he was really. But he refused when I asked for his license and even tried to come back another time, hoping another person would let him in. But I'm always here and my colleagues are vigilant too. He was most disagreeable when we stopped him."

"I imagine he was. He said he was renovating the tower?"

"Sure did. He said he was working for a Jim Redfield and we should contact him with any questions."

Liz digested this news for a moment, then asked, "Who else was looking for the plans?"

"Nancy Redfield. Pete McConnell. We know this because everyone has to sign out the documents if they want to see them, and I need to see a driver's license. We're very careful with our documents."

So basically everyone involved wanted to know what was in the clock tower. "Thank you so much, Doris. Can I get a copy mailed to me?"

"You could see if one of those people might lend theirs to you. I gave one to Kent McInerney for the renovations. Isn't he in your town? Otherwise, you have to come up here. I can't send it to you. I'm sorry, dear."

Liz said she understood and that she would check with the others before she made a trip to Indianapolis. She thanked Doris and hung up.

She mulled over who to ask first. Maybe Kent gave a copy to Jackson for the renovations when he submitted a bid for the job. She would ask Jackson in hopes of avoiding another conversation with the unpleasant developer. Things were starting to become clearer. She had another visit to make in town.

———————— //////////////////////// ————————

Liz left the inn, promising Sarah she'd be back in time for coffee hour, or so she'd hoped. None of her current guests had bothered to show up all week for it so she didn't know why she bothered. But that was part of the bed-and-breakfast package at the Olde Mansion Inn, and she had to be prepared.

She walked into Cross Furniture Company and knocked on Jackson's office door. Steve opened it and looked startled when he saw her.

"Hey, Mom. I didn't expect to see you today. How long have you been standing there?" He looked a bit nervous, but pasted a smile over it.

She had raised him since he was seven. She knew when he was hiding something.

She studied him carefully, using her patented mom stare. "What's going on, Steve? What are you up to?"

"Nothing. Just talking with Jackson about the future and options. You know, planning for when this job is done."

She didn't buy it, but decided to let him off the hook. This time. But the men in her life needed a real talking-to when this whole mess was cleared up. Steve stepped past her and headed down to his office after promising to stop by for dinner soon.

She went into the office and closed the door behind her. Jackson looked flustered and stood as soon as he saw her. "Liz, what a pleasant surprise." He kissed her on the cheek.

"I seem to be surprising a lot of people these days. What were you and Steve talking about?"

Jackson drew her over to the couch and sat down. "Like he said—the future and options. Nothing much. Why?"

"It feels like you're both keeping things from me and I wonder why. Is everything okay?"

"Of course. Why wouldn't it be?"

She didn't believe him, but she had bigger fish to fry. "Jackson, has the contractor been chosen for the tower renovation?"

He ran a hand through his hair. "No, but Kent put in an attractive bid. He has the manpower and the skills to make it happen under budget and on time. It galls me because I know he's been putting pressure on a few people to sell so he could build that development of his. It's a business practice he's always used, but we've never been able to prove it. Why do you ask?"

"Well, he went to the state archives and got the plans for the tower, saying he was in charge of the renovations. Did you give permission for that?" Liz asked.

Jackson shrugged. "He didn't need permission to get the plans. He probably wanted them so he could develop his proposal for the council."

Liz sagged against the back of the couch. *There goes that theory.* She had been positive he'd had a nefarious reason for requesting the plans. Unfortunately, he had a legitimate reason after all.

Then something Doris Tidwell had said prodded her.

"Are the Redfields involved in the renovations at all?"

"The Redfields? Why would they be involved?"

"Well, Nancy's cousin commissioned the tower. Did you ask them to work with the council on the renovations?"

He shook his head. "No, we didn't even ask them. Although,

when they came to town, Nancy and Jim came to me asking all sorts of questions about the renovations, but they did it separately."

"Didn't that seem odd to you?" Liz asked, turning over the possibilities.

He considered her words. "I guess, but no more than them coming back to a town I thought they were done with. I suppose they wouldn't have even known about the renovations or anything if you hadn't called them back here."

"I feel so guilty about that."

He put a finger under her chin and tilted her head up. "You are in no way to blame. She chose to come back here. You had offered to send the boxes to her. If she was killed, that person chose to do it. If she wasn't, she fell accidentally. Either way, it had nothing to do with you. If she hadn't come back here, would she be alive? Maybe. Maybe not. Don't put this on your shoulders, Liz. You are not to blame."

Liz bit her lower lip. "Thank you, Jackson. I've been wondering if she'd be alive today if I hadn't called her about those boxes. I couldn't help it. But until we know why and how she died, we can't know that. But I'm curious about why they poked their noses into the renovations. It had nothing to do with them since they don't live here anymore. What were they looking for?"

Jackson's brow furrowed. "Well, they asked about tower plans, the layout. And they wanted to know if there were any Clausen heirlooms found. Nancy threatened to have her lawyer file a suit in the event that we found anything belonging to the Clausens, but I have the paperwork in the town records office from when Iris donated the tower to the town. Ownership of the tower, the grounds, and all contents were transferred to the town to be kept intact as a memorial."

Liz pondered his words. "So she threatened a lawsuit against me for 'undiscovered, unnamed valuables' and she does the same for the town. Do you also get the sense she was looking for some quick money?"

He shrugged again. "You're the detective. What do you think?"

She pulled the news article out of her purse and showed it to him. "See these clocks? The article talks about these old clocks restored by Iris's father. They were valuable back when this article was published years ago. Imagine what they're worth now. I don't have any of them at the inn. I haven't found a record of them being donated with the rest of her collection of papers and odds and ends. It's possible Nancy inherited them and sold them off years ago, but what if she didn't? What if there's truth to the rumors of missing valuables in the house or the tower?"

He scanned the article, handling it carefully. Finally, he handed it back. "Is that why they were so interested in the third floor? They thought these clocks were hidden up there?"

She nodded. "I think so. That's the last place the clocks could possibly be in the house. I mean, the Redfields lived there for thirty years. They would have searched it thoroughly."

He laughed. "Unless they planned to tear it down."

She froze, staring at him. "What did you say?"

He looked confused. "Tear it down. Why?"

"How could I be so stupid!" She jumped up. "I have an idea, but I could be horribly wrong. I'll tell you about it later. Come for dinner with Steve?"

She kissed him without waiting for an answer and ran out. She had somewhere to be.

18

Liz hurried outside and then stopped. Where to begin looking for the person she needed to talk to? She knew of one way to ensure he would be where she needed him. She grabbed her cell and made a quick call, setting up a meet at the tower. He seemed irritated and rushed, but agreed to meet her within the hour. She stepped into Sweet Everything for awhile to soothe her mind and plan her next steps over a cup of coffee and one of Naomi's cranberry-orange muffins.

She arrived at the clock tower just as it chimed the hour. She headed inside and climbed the stairs to the figurine room, but he had beaten her there.

And she was too late.

He lay in the same spot where Nancy had last been seen alive. He had clearly been bludgeoned to death with the hammer that was lying next to him on the floor.

Kent McInerney was dead.

Liz gaped at him in shock and horror. She finally forced herself to do something and fumbled in her purse for her cell phone as she raced for the doorway. The killer could still be here and she needed to get out in the open. Fast.

Suddenly she was shoved back into the room. Her phone was plucked from her hand and flung at the wall, where it shattered in a cascade of plastic and metal. She whirled around and came face-to-face with Jim Redfield.

He was shaking his head. "I really wish you had stayed out of this, Liz. You're a nice person, and I hate to have to hurt you."

"You killed Kent! Why?"

He smiled, a chillingly sinister look. "No, *you* killed him when he came after you in a fit of rage, because you found out that he killed Nancy. I'm glad you called him to set up this meeting and back up my story. But sadly, you didn't survive the encounter either. What a horrible tragedy for us all."

She backed away, desperately looking for another way out of the room. She had to stall, to keep him talking as long as she could. "No one would ever believe that."

He shrugged. "If you're dead, no one will be around to refute it. They'll find the call from you on his phone's history."

"There are only so many tragic accidents that can go on before people begin to wonder."

"They can wonder all they want. They'll never figure out it was me."

"I figured it out."

He laughed. "No, you thought it was Kent. If you had waited just a little longer to get here, I would have been gone, and you would have never seen me. So, really, this is all your fault."

She glared at him; she didn't believe for a moment that he hadn't planned to frame her for Kent's death all along. "Typical. Blaming everyone else except the person really at fault—you. I didn't realize you were a sociopath, Jim."

He shook his head, advancing slowly on her, staying between her and the door, her only escape. "I'm not a sociopath, just a desperate man who is looking for what is due to me. Do you know how long I suffered at Nancy's hand while we were married? I took care of *her* relative, being treated as nothing more than a servant. Iris was kind when she was lucid, but Nancy got downright mean. Do you think Nancy would ever be a caretaker for anyone else? Of course not. She wasn't exactly the most nurturing person. Then, she decided she wanted out, to take the money and run."

He turned and began pacing in front of the door, his face red with rage. "Everyone thought our divorce was amicable and everything was split fifty-fifty, but she hid money from me. She took several antiques from the house before the sale and sold them. Do you honestly think she could afford to live as she does in Boca Raton on half of the sale from that lousy inn?"

Liz shrugged, still eyeing him warily. "I don't know how she lived or what she had saved."

"Saved!" Jim snorted. "Nancy never saved a dime in her life. She spent it all and more. I knew she had set this up years ago. She used me and she owed me. Kent was my only friend in town. He kept track of the inn, kept looking for an opportunity to buy it so we could see if there were other things hidden inside. Iris had told me about a hidden space and her father's clocks and watches, but she was delusional toward the end and couldn't tell me if it was in the house or the tower."

"So Kent is trying to buy up the land around me to force me to sell. And he waited for the tower renovation so he could shut it down and do some investigation on his own."

"Nancy hated him. She hated anyone who pulled my attention from her, and she knew he was onto her. She wouldn't sell to him, and then you came along with your better offer, and she took it like that." He snapped his fingers. "When you found that room, I tried to have you hire him to do the work, but you refused. When nothing was in that room, we figured it had to be in the tower."

A realization dawned. "You found it. You found the hidden room."

A crafty look crossed his face and he glared at her. "Kent found it a few days ago, I guess, and never told me. He's been slowly chipping away at a piece to make a hole big enough for a camera. But it's walled up tight and deep. I overheard Kent's conversation with you on the phone and knew you'd probably figured it out."

"Why did you kill Nancy? Why couldn't you just get into the room, get whatever's inside, and head out with no one the wiser?" Liz had backed up until she reached the waist-high fence surrounding the figurines. She gripped the edge of the fence and kept her eyes tightly fixed on Jim.

For the first time, he looked regretful. "I didn't mean to kill her. That was truly an accident. We were arguing in here and she pushed me. It just made me think of how she pushed me around for years. I wasn't going to take another minute of it. I pushed her back, and she stumbled against the fence and fell over. Almost in the same spot where you're standing now."

A chill ran up Liz's spine, and she tried to move, but Jim was too close. Panic was setting in, and she tried to push it down so she could think clearly. Why had she rushed out of Jackson's office without telling him where she was going?

"You can't tell me Kent was an accident too."

"He shouldn't have double-crossed me. I don't like betrayal," he said, as if that were a perfectly reasonable excuse for murder. "Now, how to take care of you?"

"If someone else goes over the same way as Nancy, they'll know it's not an accident," Liz said, thinking fast. "You could say you killed Kent in self-defense. As you said, no one would know any different. Nancy fell. It wasn't your fault."

He shook his head. "I hit Kent on the back of the head. I doubt anyone would believe self-defense if he was facing away from me."

She inched her way along the fence toward a wall. "They won't believe it of me either. For the same reason." She injected a note of pleading into her voice, hoping to reason with him as she inched sideways. "Jim, you don't want to do this. Please."

"I'm sorry, Liz. I have to. I need her insurance money and whatever is in that room. Don't worry. I'll make it quick."

Liz saw her chance. She threw her large purse in his face and bolted for the door, hoping to throw him off balance and give herself a split-second chance to get away. But his hand closed around her upper arm, and he yanked her back. He locked her in place with a steel grip and one hand over her mouth and nose. Liz struggled for breath as he blocked her airways.

"I really wish you hadn't done that." He dragged her toward the figurines.

She kicked and struggled, but he was too strong. She tried letting her body go limp to make it more difficult for him to move her, but to no avail.

"Sorry, Liz," he said. "I'm sure you'll be missed around here."

He pressed her against the fence, and she lost all hope.

The door flew open, slamming against the stone wall, and Jackson and Stan burst in, Stan's gun trained on Liz's captor. "Freeze, Jim. Let her go."

Jim's grip loosened enough for her to tear herself away, gasping for breath. Jackson pulled her across the room, away from Jim, while Stan cuffed the man and read him his rights. Liz buried her head in Jackson's shoulder while he held her close, his chin resting on her head.

"You know," Jackson said, "you'd have fewer close calls if you didn't just leave me to guess at what you were thinking when you crack a case. Just a thought."

"I'll keep that in mind."

19

Liz gratefully accepted a cup of heavily sweetened coffee from Jackson, who then sat next to her on the couch in Stan's office. He seemed unable to leave her side, as if reassuring himself that she was safe and wouldn't disappear. She sagged against the back of the couch, sipping the hot liquid and feeling it chase away the chill that had permeated her whole body since the attack.

The door opened and Stan came in, closing it behind him. He sat in one of the chairs. "I'm sorry, Liz. Kent is dead too. Probably instantaneous from the hammer. Jim hit him just right."

"I guess I'm lucky he didn't still have it in his hand when I came in the room." Liz laughed, the sound shaky to her ears.

Jackson shook his head. "Don't even joke about that, Liz. Thank God I decided to follow you when I saw you heading for the tower."

"I'm sorry I didn't tell you what I was doing." She gripped his hand. "I'm so glad you came in when you did."

Her eyes filled as the reality of the situation hit her afresh. She blinked rapidly, trying to refocus. "What has Jim said, Stan?"

"We already were watching him, Liz. He had gambling debts, lots of them. A windfall from a life insurance policy could go a long way to solving that problem."

"I'm still surprised Nancy kept him as her beneficiary," Liz said.

Stan shrugged. "She had no one else, and I doubt she expected to die this young. He swears it was an accident, and I doubt we can prove otherwise, but we definitely have him for Kent's murder and your attempted murder. He thought Kent was going to steal the treasure for himself. If there even was a treasure."

"Do we know where the room is? Maybe we could open it and see what this is all about," said Liz.

For the first time since Liz was attacked, Jackson smiled. "You and your secret rooms."

"I hate secrets, especially when they lead to murder," she replied.

Jackson held up his hand. "I'll check with the council, but I'm sure they'll be okay with seeing if Kent was onto something. It's part of the town's history, and we could use the exposure if something is found. It might even be a tourist draw. I'll set up the demolition for tomorrow."

"Liz, how did you know it was Jim?" Stan asked.

"I didn't, although I thought he was involved somehow. I honestly thought it was Kent, because he was so insistent on me selling the inn to him and on being involved here at the tower. And he and Jim seemed to be so close. But I never even suspected it was Jim."

She leaned back against the couch and sipped her coffee. "I called Kent and set up a meeting. Jim overheard Kent's conversation with me, and he knew Kent had been working at opening the secret room. That's when he decided to set me up for the murder, like he tried to set up Sadie."

Jackson gaped at her. "You set up a meeting alone with someone you suspected was a murderer? Never again. Promise me you'll stay out of murders from now on. I have so many gray hairs from you."

She smiled. "I'll try."

Stan stood. "Stay as long as you need to. I have to finish questioning Jim and process him for arrest." He left, closing the door behind him.

Liz laid her head on Jackson's shoulder. She felt safe, protected. But curiosity burned inside. What was in that room? Was it really worth killing over? She couldn't wait to find out. But first, she needed a long bath to soothe her aching muscles from her tangle with Jim.

———— ⁓⁓⁓⁓⁓⁓⁓⁓ ————

Jackson moved fast when he needed to. The next day, local stonemasons showed up at the tower and carefully broke down the section of wall Kent had begun to work on. Melissa Patton was also there, an air of barely suppressed eagerness around her. It took most of the morning to get a spot opened up enough to see inside, during which Liz weeded in the garden plot and enjoyed the warmth of the sun.

Finally, Jackson called to her, "We're almost there. Come inside."

Liz brushed her hands on her jeans, doing her best to clean off the dirt, and hurried inside to finally see what the whole mess was about.

Stone chips littered the floor, and the noise from the chisels was deafening. Jackson handed her a headset to muffle the sound and protect her ears. A section of the wall collapsed and the masons stepped away. Jackson gestured to Liz.

"You're the one who almost died for this. It's only fair that you're the first to see inside."

She switched on the powerful flashlight Jackson handed her and shined it inside the dark room. A wooden table sat in the middle of the room, a tea set laid out on the top with a service for two. Two simple wooden chairs sat on either side of the table.

Every other piece of furniture in the room was covered with antique clocks, even more than were shown in the article picture. Liz sucked in a breath at the sight and started coughing at the dust that came with it. She pulled away and gratefully accepted the bottle of water Jackson offered her.

"Well?"

She handed Jackson the flashlight. "See for yourself."

Slowly, the flashlight was passed around to everyone and they all had a chance to see. Then Jackson instructed everyone to step away, and the masons finished demolishing the wall. Later that day, they were officially able to walk fully into the room, after it had been cleared by a local environmentalist. What Liz had seen was even more impressive by the light of the huge lamps set up by the workmen.

It was a small room, maybe twelve feet square, situated under the stairs where Liz and Pete had first suspected. It looked as if Iris had laid out an entire shrine to her father, with a picture of him surrounded by the most elegant clocks. Her tea set had been lovingly arranged on the table. It was an expensive set made of bone china that was so delicate Liz was afraid to touch it. It was a memorial, a dedication to the father Iris had loved.

Jackson leaned down and whispered, "Is this worth killing over?"

She shook her head. "Nothing is worth killing over. But this should be preserved. These pieces are part of her family's legacy. And only one person is alive who can guide us on how it should be handled."

He quirked a brow at her. "Who is that? Jim?"

"No. Her grandson." She turned and gestured to the man standing outside the door hesitantly. "This is your history, Pete. Your great-grandfather loved this collection of clocks, and your grandmother preserved it. You have more right to be here than any of us."

He stared around the room, eyes wide and glistening a bit. "You believe me?"

Jackson grinned. "She tends to be right about this kind of thing."

Melissa gaped at him. "You're Iris Clausen's heir? I have so many questions for you! Will you let us document this room and write about it?"

He nodded. "Yes, definitely."

She rubbed her hands together with excitement. "Oh, I can't wait to dive into this."

Melissa began to take notes and sketch the room on a notepad, consulting with Pete. Liz smiled at the sight of them working together, just as their forebears, the architect Charles Lawrence and the patroness Iris Clausen, had done to create the beautiful tower they now stood in.

Jackson jutted his chin toward a journal lying on a desk. "Dare we open it?"

Liz shook her head. "We should let an expert do that. Someone who knows how to handle paper and all of these pieces without damaging them. And I'll bet someone at the state historical society can advise us."

"I defer to your judgment, since you were one of the discoverers."

They walked out of the room and tower, and into the garden. She still felt as if there was something unspoken between her and Jackson. She'd have to deal with that soon. But how to approach it?

———————

The next morning, Liz decided it was high time to look through those boxes. She carried them one by one into the library, then began to sort.

But all that was there were pictures, letters, and journals. There were no clocks, no money—nothing that would be considered treasure, at least not the monetary kind.

Liz sat on the floor and continued sorting through the documents. She tried to find some kind of order at first, but quickly gave up and just put pictures in one pile, letters in another, and books and journals in a third pile. After an hour, Sarah brought some refreshments on a tray to give Liz a break. She stayed to help with the rest of the items.

When they'd finished, Liz stood and studied the piles, hands on her hips. Now, what to do? She was technically the owner. Actually, she had always been the owner, but, since she had insisted on being nice, these boxes had created a lot of havoc in a lot of people's lives. She'd have to go through the contents more thoroughly. She'd definitely consider looping Bert Worth in. He'd recognize anything of historical value better than she would, and his knowledge of area history and his status as amateur historian made him the ideal candidate to curate this material, if it was even worth it.

She decided to start with the journals and opened the first one, noting what looked to her like a woman's handwriting. The initials *IAC* were engraved on the cover—Iris Anne Clausen. A chill ran up her spine and she started reading.

The sun had almost set by the time Liz finished skimming the journals and going through the letters. Sarah had brought her lunch and left her to read in peace in the easy chair in the room. Liz closed the last journal and was surprised to find her face streaked with tears. How Jim or Nancy could not think these were valuable was beyond her. They were insight into a woman who had devoted herself to her family and her father, had sacrificed her own happiness to care for her ailing parent, had lost a child, and always had the love of her life near her, but had never been able to marry him. She was a product of her times, and the situation was so sad. Liz had no right to judge.

But it was clear that Iris had loved Michael McConnell and he had loved her, staying with her until the end. They'd remained in contact with their son's adoptive parents, sending money and support as they could until Iris's death, when Michael had left to live with Pete's family. Iris had received letters and pictures of her son growing up. She had remained in contact with him, without ever seeing him in person or being able to touch him, which made Liz understandably sad. It made her think of Steve and his parents, who had died when he was so young. They hadn't been able to watch him grow up, hadn't experienced any of his milestones, but she hoped in some sense they knew what a fine man he'd become.

A sound from the stairway made Liz jerk out of her thoughts. She stiffly got out of the chair went into the rotunda. Someone was heading up to the third floor. Only Pete was staying up there, and he was just the person she wanted to see.

She went to the stairs and called up to him. "Pete? Can you come down here? I have something I think you need to see."

He trotted back down, a questioning look on his face. She led him to the library. "Iris Clausen saved pictures and letters about your father. She watched over him growing up. She even wrote about him in her journal. I thought you might like to look at what she saved."

He stared at the pile of stuff on the bed and floor, clearly overwhelmed as Liz handed him a picture of his father as a baby in Iris's arms, with Michael McConnell standing next to them. It was a picture of a family that was soon torn apart. He blinked rapidly and sniffled as he looked through a stack of pictures of his father.

"She loved him."

Liz nodded. "She truly did."

"I know she couldn't have kept him, even though she had money."

Liz sat on the edge of the bed, and repeated his own earlier words back to him. "It was a different time, Pete. Her father would have never approved of a match between her and your grandfather. And her father needed her. It had been just her and her father since her mother died when she was very young. She couldn't leave him, and she couldn't take care of him and a baby. Plus, her having a baby out of wedlock would have shamed him."

"It's still hard to get past this, although I've thought about it enough."

Liz shook her head sadly. "She wasn't raised that way, Pete. She had been close to her neighbors, the Bielers. Their eldest, Samuel, had fallen in love with a woman who was not Amish, and he wanted to leave the Amish and Pleasant Creek. She offered him money and support to raise your father, which they did. They agreed to an open adoption—very unusual at the time—and provided updates as the baby grew, letting him keep his real father's last name. She sent them money, especially after Samuel Bieler's death in the war. The Clausen fortune was never as vast as people thought, and she spent most of it to make sure your father was well provided for."

"Why didn't my grandfather leave?"

"How could he leave the woman he loved, even if they could never be married? When the Redfields came, that must have been when Iris asked him to seal up the tower room. He could have taken the clocks, but I guess he didn't since we found the tower room preserved the way it was."

"She was supposed to have left him money. The Redfields made sure he never got that." Pete's voice was bitter.

"That's on them, not your grandmother. She did her best for your father and grandfather." Liz stood. "I really think you should read her journals and look through the letters. And I want you to keep them. They're your history. There are a couple of pictures of this house and the original owners that I might want to display here at the inn, but I can have copies made."

He looked up at her, eyes shining. "You have no idea what this means to me. You've found my history, my family. And you're being so kind."

Liz bit her lip, then said hesitantly, "Technically, this inn is your ancestral home."

Pete grinned. "I have a place of my own, Liz. I can see how much you love the inn. I'd never challenge you for ownership. Besides, the Redfields inherited the place from my grandmother per her will, and you bought it from them fair and square. The Olde Mansion Inn is yours for as long as you want it, though I'd love to come back and visit from time to time, to feel close to my family. You gave me my family history selflessly, even though you didn't know what I might want to do with it. For all you knew, I could have turned out like Nancy and tried to cheat you out of everything I could get my hands on. Thank you, Liz. You've given me a priceless gift and I won't forget it."

He hugged her, and she blinked back tears. "It was my pleasure. I'll bring you a sandwich up here so you can start reading the papers if you'd like. And then, tomorrow, I can take you over to the Bielers' farm to meet them. Samuel's nephew still works on the farm, and I think he'd like to meet you. You may not have been a blood relative, but I think he'd like to know you even so. They're good people."

Pete nodded. "Thank you."

She left the room as Pete slowly sank into the chair, still staring at the pictures, his face showing how overwhelmed he was by the information in front of him.

Jackson quietly stood in the hallway, waiting for her. "You did a good thing, Liz. He needed those answers."

Liz smiled and led Jackson downstairs, suddenly feeling horribly tired. She went into the kitchen and made tea for herself and Jackson. "It's his heritage. He deserves to know."

"He might be angry that she didn't keep his father to raise herself," Jackson said.

"He was a little hurt about it when I talked to him. Maybe the journal will help. Maybe it won't. But at least he can hear it from her lips, so to speak." She sat at the kitchen table with him.

"Are you sure he won't challenge you for ownership of the inn, based on whether the Redfields had the right to sell it?"

She shook her head. "No, I had my new attorney check into the Clausen will to ensure the Redfields had the right to sell it. According to the only will on record, she gave the house to the Redfields for taking care of her for the last couple of years of her life."

"And you believe it?" Jackson asked.

"I don't know what to believe, but I don't really have a choice. Could they have duped her into giving them the house? Sure. I'm still not clear on how they're related since Iris had no other children and no siblings, and Nancy was a distant cousin. And she couldn't exactly leave it to her secret son and his descendants without someone finding out who he was."

"Why not leave it to Michael McConnell, the love of her life and the man who stood by her with no reward? He never got to show the world he loved her, never lived as her husband, yet he stayed with her until the end."

Liz shook her head. "According to her journal, he was a proud man. He was the one who didn't want to marry her and cause trouble with the family. He never thought he was good enough. So he refused to accept anything from her estate. Maybe that's why he never fought the Redfields on the money he was owed."

"It seems pointless and sad, you know. Pride and duty before love and family."

"To Iris, they were all the same. She was torn in two between the family she had in her father and the family she wanted in Michael."

He nodded. "At least Pete has his grandmother's papers. Oh, and I forgot to tell you. They found an old pocket watch in the teapot in the tower room, and we think it belonged to Michael McConnell, based on the inscription. We'll give it to Pete."

Liz smiled. "That's perfect. I'm so glad. He deserves something from his family."

"So, what's next for you?"

"Well, I've given Pete the boxes, and tomorrow I'll introduce him to the Bielers. We'll see where it goes from there."

Jackson nodded. "We're checking on the donation and Iris's will.

I don't want to exclude Pete, nor do we want to sell anything. But if he thinks he'll just take everything in the room and sell it, well, we might fight him. I don't believe he has any legal claim."

Liz shook her head. "I don't think he'll do that. I think he'll stick to what he said and leave it here. I wouldn't be surprised if he moves here. He has no other family. Maybe Pleasant Creek could become his home."

"Taking in more strays, Liz?" Jackson teased.

She shrugged. "If he needs it."

Jackson stood and hugged her. "You're a good woman, Liz Eckardt. We're lucky to have you here. I have to run. Lots to do before the garden-tour opening tomorrow. See you there?"

She nodded and walked him out. He left without even kissing her goodbye.

When had things gotten so awkward between them, and how could she fix it?

20

Liz, the Material Girls, and other business owners who had donated flowers and labor to make the garden plots gathered at the tower garden to officially open the season and welcome tourists to the town.

The clock tower was technically closed for renovations, especially in light of the discovery of the secret room. The council was considering an outside firm for the job, but for now, they didn't want people traipsing in and out of the space and trying to get into the room with its fragile artifacts. An antiques expert had come in to help preserve everything and promised to share updates as he had them.

For now, the gardens, the clock's chimes, and the dancing figurines would have to suffice. It would do, and the story of the discovery of the secret room would keep attracting people into next season and beyond. Liz sensed a theme coming on for upcoming seasons. But for now, these quilts made of flowers would suffice.

Several dignitaries spoke on the history of the town and the tower and the garden, including a mention of the Clausen family, who were getting some long-overdue recognition.

Pete McConnell had been thrust reluctantly into the spotlight, although he avoided the speeches for that day. For a man who only wanted to know about his history, he was struggling a bit, not being used to the attention. He had connected with the Bielers. In fact, he was staying with them and considering remaining with them long-term. He was never going to become Amish, but he might consider becoming a farmer. The point was, he now had a family, even with both of his parents deceased, and he was happy to have a place to belong.

Jackson finished his speech but didn't initially make his way over to her. Instead, he stood talking with Melissa Patton and a few other people.

"Hey, Mom." She turned to see Steve standing next to her, a bottle of water in his hand. "Nice job on the garden. I can't believe you helped do this. You always killed plants when I was growing up."

She grinned wryly. "I didn't do that much. Sadie and Mary Ann and the other Material Girls did most of the work. And I just followed Sadie's directions when I was here."

He pulled back slightly and studied her. "You're really happy here, aren't you? When you said you were moving to a small town in Indiana, I couldn't believe it. This is so far from Boston, as far as it could be in a lot of ways. But now that I see you here, I think I get it."

She stared out at the crowd of people—people who, two years ago, were complete strangers to her. Sadie, Mary Ann, Opal, Naomi, Caitlyn. These were the Material Girls who barged into her shop one morning and into her life, pulling her into their circle and becoming her friends, closer than almost anyone else she had ever known. Then she found her mother's family—her family, including Miriam who had become like a sister to her. Her eyes found Jackson again and her smile softened.

She sighed. "Yes, this is home now, and I love it here. It's completely different from the big city, but it's exactly where I need to be and I feel like I'm who I want to be here." She laid a hand on his arm. "You don't have to stay though. I understand this may not be the right place for a young man like you. You have your whole life ahead of you. Make your own choices, Steve. I'll always be here."

He grinned. "Well, I haven't made any firm decisions, and it's true that Pleasant Creek isn't exactly a hotbed of fun for a young guy like me. But I find it suits me, at least for now. I like the quiet, the slower pace. Boston has become a little too much for me. When I was there

I kept feeling on edge, jumpy, as if I was back in Kosovo. But here, I can relax. I know the job with Cross Furniture will be over soon, but I was dabbling in some of the woodworking with a couple of guys in the shop. I'm not sure if it will be the career for me, but I do like working with my hands."

"I remember that you enjoyed taking shop classes in school. I'm not surprised at all. I'm glad you're liking it here. But remember, if you ever decide this isn't for you, I'll understand."

"Don't worry, Mom. I'll let you know. Are we still on for dinner tonight?" He sounded so eager, like a little kid.

She hugged him, never tired of being able to touch him and know he was safe. "Absolutely."

"Great, can we make it a bit later, though? Like seven?"

"Sure, that works for me. But why so late?"

He shrugged. "I just have something to finish up. Is that okay?"

"Of course. See you then."

He wandered off and the Material Girls came over, chatting about their garden, all congratulating Mary Ann on her design.

"So simple, but the colors coordinate perfectly, Mary Ann. Excellent job on the design. We're sure to at least place this year in the competition," Opal said.

"I hope so. We've certainly worked hard enough. And the colors *are* perfect. So vibrant and sharp. Now, if only they can stay that way," Sadie said.

Naomi's sharp eyes studied Liz. "Is everything okay, Liz?"

All of the women's eyes turned to her, peeling back the layers of her facade until she was laid bare in front of them. "I don't know. I think you might be right about Jackson."

They all exchanged glances. Finally, Naomi cleared her throat. "We can't do this here. Let's go to the bakery."

They headed down the street and into the bakery. Naomi set cups for tea or coffee in front of everyone and gave them generous slices of coffee cake. When everyone was served, she sat and fixed Liz with a stern stare.

"Start from the beginning."

"Well, you all started it. Naomi, you saw Jackson with Sally, and we know the only reason he'd talk to her was if he was selling or buying real estate. I can't imagine he'd be buying anything, so he must be selling. And what could that be? I know he's going into the city frequently, and he's taken out a business loan because things are tough at the factory. He is not hiring, and he's losing staff."

"So, he's going through a tough time. He needs you to stand by him," Mary Ann said.

"And I've tried to do just that, but he brushes me off, refuses to share with me. I can't understand why he won't trust me, won't let me in. I thought we were more than just friends."

"You know, relationships are not always roses and fun times. They take faith, trust, and work. This might be one of those times." Mary Ann said gently.

Liz stared at her. "I'm trying, but I feel like he's shutting me out."

The women stared at each other in dismay and rushed to comfort her. They spent the next couple of hours trying to convince her that she was wrong, but no one could come up with a reasonable explanation for Liz. Finally, she glanced at the time and jumped to her feet.

"I have to get going if I'm going to make dinner for Steve."

"Honey, why don't you cancel that for tonight. Get some rest instead," Caitlyn suggested.

She shook her head. "No, I could use the distraction. Thank you all so much. I'll be better tomorrow. You've been great."

Naomi hugged her. "Want me to walk you home?"

Liz shook her head. "I can handle it. Thanks."

Liz hugged them all and headed out of the bakery. Dusk was settling in. Her friends had meant well and had tried to comfort her, but she wasn't ready.

She walked the short distance to the inn and thought about Jackson. About them. Her friends were right. She had to have faith in him. Relationships were about faith and trust in each other. Jackson, like Liz, wasn't used to having someone else to rely on. Maybe he didn't know yet how to open up and share. And here she was walking away. No, he deserved more than that from her. Their relationship deserved more.

She stood up, her decision made. Now that her inn was empty of guests for a couple of days, she would invite Jackson over for dinner tomorrow and talk to him, really talk to him. They'd work this out. It was too important.

Liz was about to open the front door when Beans came around from the back and gave a little bark. Strangely, her dog was wearing a bright-red bow tie around his pudgy neck. Where in the world had that come from? And what was he doing outside?

He looked a bit put upon, as if he was suffering the ultimate indignity, which she guessed he was.

"How did you get out of the house? Who dressed you up, Beans?"

As soon as she got close to him, he turned and trotted down the walkway and around the house toward Jaynes Lake and the gazebo. Liz hurried after him, not understanding why Beans was out and running away from her. As she was about to turn the corner, someone stood there. She stopped abruptly, and Steve held up his hand.

"Hi, Mom. It's just me."

She laid a hand on her chest, her heart pounding a little from being startled. "Steve, I didn't expect you so early. I just need to get Beans and then I can get started on dinner."

He smiled, a mysterious half-smile. "I won't be able to stay for dinner. I'm sorry. But I'll help you find Beans. Here, let me help you." He held out his arm in an oddly formal gesture and she took it. He tucked her hand in the crook of his arm as if he were escorting her to a formal event, and he stepped around the corner of the house.

The rest of the walkway was lined with different-colored lights in paper bags, casting a light glow in the dusk, guiding her way down a path toward the gazebo. She let her gaze follow the illuminated path until they reached the gazebo. She gasped.

The gazebo had been decorated with white lights all around the spindles and the roof. It twinkled like stars in the night sky, casting a glow in the rapidly darkening night. Standing in the opening to the gazebo was Jackson.

He wore dress pants and a blazer, hands folded in front of him, feet shoulder width apart, as he solemnly gazed down the path toward her, waiting patiently. He was tense and still. Beans, the traitor, had made his choice, sitting at Jackson's feet, panting slightly but watching.

Steve had paused, letting her absorb the whole scene. Finally, she started breathing again, and he patted her hand.

"Are you okay?" he asked.

"What's going on?"

"You're going to have to walk over there to find out. I'm just here to help you along the way in case you need it. Or help you leave. It's your choice. What do you want?"

Her head spun with shock and she clung to Steve for balance as she tried to comprehend. He stood there patiently, lending her his strength. Finally, she heaved a deep breath.

"I'm ready." She took a step forward, somehow understanding that she was heading to a moment that was going to irrevocably change her life.

As she got closer to Jackson, she saw his eyes widen and his shoulders ease slightly under his blazer. They reached the bottom step of the gazebo and Steve released her arm. He turned and embraced her.

"Thank you for being the best mom a guy could ever have. Go have the life you were meant to have." He kissed her lightly on the cheek. In a low whisper, he added, "He's a good guy."

She smiled and hugged him back. "I love you, Steve."

He gave Jackson a nod and turned on his heel with military precision, then double-timed it around the corner of the house, Beans on his tail.

Liz looked at Jackson. "Bologna?"

A faint smile crossed his face. "Steve has five slices in his pocket."

She nodded. Jackson held out his hand and led her up the stairs and into the gazebo. A table had been laid out with a series of appetizers on it, along with wine. He pulled out a chair and settled Liz in it.

"It was such a beautiful night, I thought we could sit outside."

She arched her eyebrow. "You wanted to invite me to dinner?"

He twisted his hands in front of him, nerves clearly getting the better of him. He shook his head. "No, I wanted to do this."

He got down on one knee next to her chair. "Liz, I had just about given up on finding that special someone to spend the rest of my life with, and then you came along. I had settled into bachelorhood, working all day, being alone at night. Then I met you and you brought lightness and love and laughter into my life. You also brought a little stress with the crimes and dead bodies, but I can overlook that, as long as you watch out for your safety."

She laughed, surprised to find her face wet with tears. "I promise to watch out and not get involved in any more murders, if I can help it."

"I'd appreciate it. My heart can't take it, and I'm not getting any younger." He sucked in a shaky breath. "Anyway, I've been trying to line up everything and give it to you in a neat little package. But I now realize that all you need is for me to speak from the heart."

"What do you mean?"

"Liz, I want you to marry me. I love you and I want to spend the rest of my life with you." He held up his hand. "Before you say anything, I need to explain some things. I don't want you to give up the inn unless you want to. I could live here. My house is really no more than a bachelor pad anyway, and I've talked with Sally Van Amburgh about putting it on the market."

She closed her eyes and opened them, not sure what was coming next.

"I been going into the city so often, not for business or bank loans, but to find this."

He opened a blue velvet box to show an antique diamond ring with ornate silver filigree. Liz sucked in a breath and reached a tentative hand out to touch it, then hesitated, looking up at him, eyes wide. "Are you serious?"

"Dead serious." Then he grimaced at his choice of words. "Sorry. But yes, marry me, Liz."

She blinked rapidly, dashing away tears from her face, laughing and crying at the same time. "Yes, Jackson. I'll marry you. I love you, you know." Now that she said the words, she knew it too.

He slipped the ring on her finger and stood, pulling her close into a tight hug, kissing her to seal the deal. "Now, you can't get away. You're mine, forever. And I love you too. I think I have loved you since the day I met you."

He turned his head and raised his voice, "You can all come out now."

Steve, Beans, and the Material Girls all emerged from the other side of the house, tentative grins on their faces. "She said yes!"

Relief spread on the Material Girls' faces and they all cheered, rushing across the grass to hug both Jackson and Liz, and to offer their congratulations. There were tears, laughter, and barking all around.

Liz had thought she was starting a new life when she moved to Pleasant Creek. But now, she understood that her time here had only been a lead-up to this moment.

And she could hardly wait to see what the future held.

Learn more about Annie's fiction books at

AnniesFiction.com

We've designed the Annie's Fiction website especially for you!

Access your e-books • Read sample chapters • Manage your account

Choose from one of these great series:

Amish Inn Mysteries

Annie's Attic Mysteries

Annie's Mysteries Unraveled

Annie's Quilted Mysteries

Annie's Secrets of the Quilt

Antique Shop Mysteries

Chocolate Shoppe Mysteries

Creative Woman Mysteries

Hearts of Amish Country

Secrets of the Castleton Manor Library

Victorian Mansion Flower Shop Mysteries

What are you waiting for? Visit us now at **AnniesFiction.com!**